More Letters FROM Pemberley

1814–1819

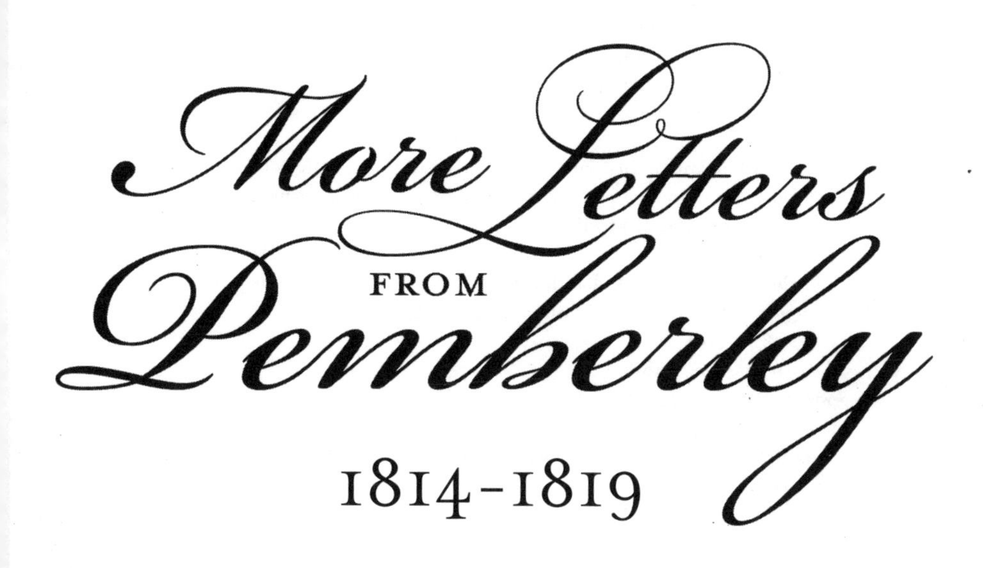

A novel of sisters, husbands, heirs

JANE DAWKINS

Published by Sourcebooks Landmark, an imprint of Sourcebooks, Inc.
P.O. Box 4410, Naperville, Illinois 60567–4410
(630) 961–3900
FAX: (630) 961–2168
www.sourcebooks.com

Originally published by iUniverse, Inc. (ISBN 0595283721) © 2003 by Jane Dawkins

Library of Congress Cataloging-in-Publication Data
Dawkins, Jane
More letters from Pemberley, 1814-1819 : a novel of sisters, husbands, heirs / Jane Dawkins.
p. cm.

ISBN-10: 1-4022-0907-X (trade pbk.)
ISBN-13: 978-1-4022-0907-9 (trade pbk.)
1. Bennet, Elizabeth (Fictitious character)—Fiction. 2. Darcy, Fitzwilliam (Fictitious character)—Fiction. 3. England—Social life and customs—19th century—Fiction. I. Austen, Jane, 1775-1817. Pride and prejudice. II. Title.
PS3554.A9458M67 2007
813'.54—dc22
2007022865

Printed and bound in the United States of America
VP 10 9 8 7 6 5 4 3 2 1

To the readers of

Letters from Pemberley

who asked for more …

… and to my husband, Charles,

who made it possible

Letter writing is the only device for
combining solitude with good company.

—George Gordon, Lord Byron

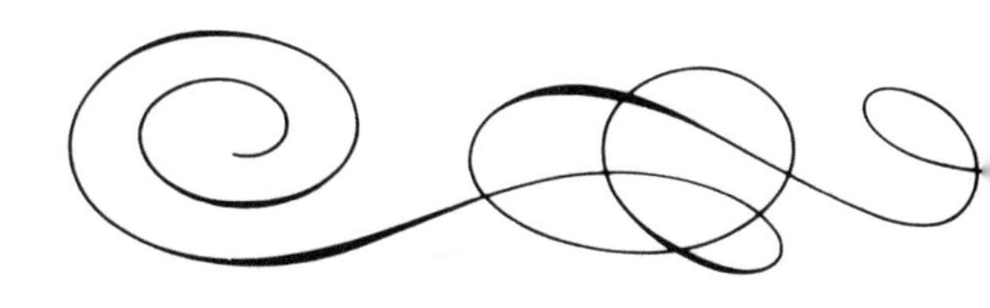

Table of Contents

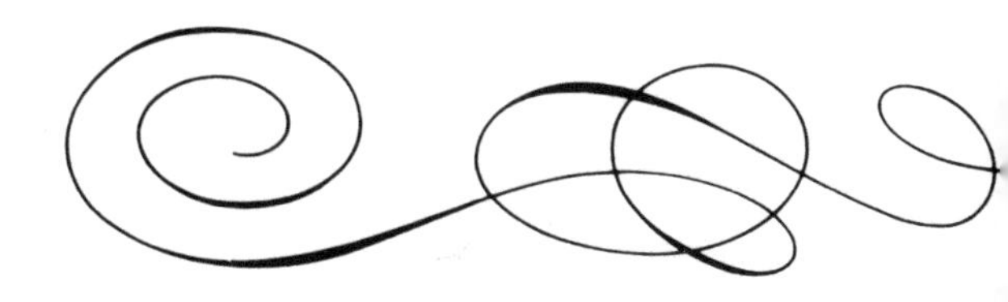

Acknowledgements

First and always, to Jane Austen, whose prose never stales and continues to inspire.

Thanks to Charles Newton of the Victoria and Albert Museum in London for his help with painters of the period … and to Barry Fitzgerald for his help, expertise and friendship.

I am also indebted to Margaret Campilonga for her unstinting support and unwavering enthusiasm for this book and to Deb Werksman, Susie Benton and Rebecca Kilbreath at Sourcebooks for all their support, enthusiasm and hard work.

Lastly, my thanks, love and appreciation to my husband, Chuck, for continuing to save me from the perils of the dark computer abyss, and supporting me in every way.

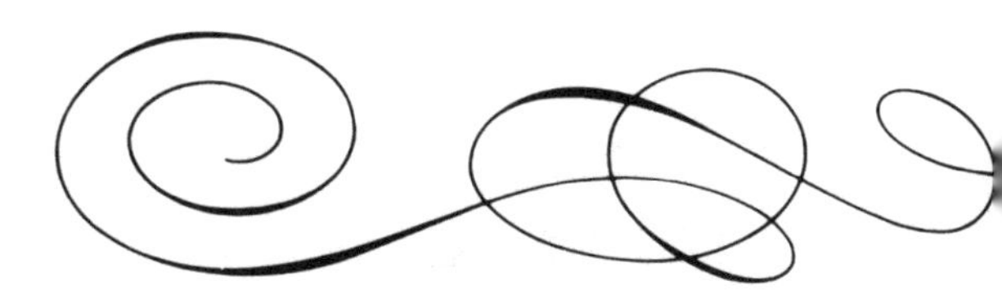

Introduction

After writing *Letters from Pemberley* I thought I was done with the Bennets and Darcys and planned to move on to other things. It was something of a surprise to be asked so often for more, and initially I would respond that sorry, I had nothing more to say on the subject.

Re-reading Jane Austen's last book, *Persuasion*, (like *Northanger Abbey*, published after her death in 1817) made me think again. In Anne Elliott, Miss Austen gives us a very different, more mature heroine than those in her earlier books. In her late twenties, Anne has had more experience of the world and of the disappointments life brings to each of us along the way. It is tantalising to wonder about the women Jane Austen might have written about in future books had not her life been cut so tragically short.

It was this conjecture that led me to think about the woman Elizabeth Bennet might have matured into as Mrs. Darcy. No longer a girl or a newly-wed, mindful of her duties as a wife and mistress of Pemberley (and, like every other woman of her station and time, imbued with the paramount duty to produce an heir) surely this mantle of responsibility would have added a little gravitas to the Lizzy we all love in *Pride and Prejudice*? This intriguing thought has finally resulted in *More Letters from Pemberley*.

The Regency period ends in 1820 after the death of George III, when the Prince Regent finally assumes the throne as George IV. After that time begins a period of great change and social unrest in England which affects all parts of society, among them Reform (of Parliament) and the Industrial Revolution, which is gathering momentum at an astonishing speed. In her first five novels Jane Austen barely mentions the great issue of her day, the Napoleonic Wars, even though with two brothers in the Royal Navy, it was a subject of great personal interest. Not until her final novel, *Persuasion*, does the Royal Navy take a more prominent role. Had she lived into the 1820s and 1830s, she could hardly have avoided having her characters feel the effects of the changes taking place around them, very close to home (especially in Derbyshire, a major centre of the Industrial Revolution!)

With the best will in the world I cannot imagine our Lizzy in the new crinoline fashions of the late 1820s and 1830s, any more than I wish to record Mr. Darcy dealing with the problems which would undoubtedly have arisen when his tenants began to leave the fields in search of wealth in the new northern factories. I will gladly leave those to other pens to describe, and unashamedly choose to leave the Darcys and Bennets at the close of 1819 still in the comfortable, familiar territory of the Regency where we first met them.

Nevertheless, I freely concede that this is not a book Jane Austen might have written. I have made a conscious decision to include the sometimes unpleasant realities of everyday life which would have affected even a family as privileged as the Darcys, and in so doing beg the reader's indulgence.

Like *Letters from Pemberley*, this book is another patchwork, drawing on Jane Austen's novels and letters for a delicious line here, a waspish phrase there, and the odd Austen dart delivered with astonishing accuracy to firmly skewer its target. I hope that my attempt to honour her succeeds in entertaining her devoted readers.

Jane Dawkins
Key West, Florida

1814

PEMBERLEY

WEDNESDAY, 12th JANUARY, 1814

My dear Aunt Gardiner,

My pen might prefer to tell you that the demands of the Christmas festivities here at Pemberley allowed me not a minute to write, not even to a much loved Aunt. Indeed, a clever paragraph or two might even persuade you to feel sorry for me—but my heart will have none of it. I have neglected you abominably these past weeks, and any sorrow you have should be for yourself alone in having such a selfish creature for a Niece.

Let me assure you that we are all well. Jane and Mr. Bingley have left us and returned to The Great House on 27th last. (You have probably heard that my Sister is very well pleased with her new home and finds nothing to contradict our report to her last August. You and I may, I think, congratulate ourselves on our part in the business.) My Mother and Father, Kitty and Mary joined them yesterday. I flatter myself that their time at Pemberley passed not unpleasantly, and trust that they shared some of my own considerable pleasure at having our family together again.

But what of Mr. Darcy's pleasure, I hear you ask? Indeed, he bore the burden of a houseful of Bennets exceedingly well. If there were some days when he and Mr. Bingley (and sometimes my Father) were absent from home longer than might be expected, I did not notice it; if there were other times when Mr. Darcy and my Father removed themselves to the library for lengthy periods, let it just be said that Mr. Darcy has a high regard for my Father's opinion and would naturally wish to discuss with him continuing improvements and other matters of a bibliographical nature.

We have had some merry parties here and were joined at various times by Lady Ashton Dennis, the Mansfields, Norlands and dear Eleanor Steventon, who entertained us with stories—often at her own expense—about life in Bath (though I suspect the stories are more amusing in the telling than in the reality). The Daleys, sadly, were obliged to stay at home. Mrs. Daley's father has been confined to bed with a severe cold for several weeks and she is loath to leave him. Anna and Fanny Norland stayed with us almost a week, insufficient time for Kitty and Fanny to run out of conversation, which was often accompanied by peals of laughter. Anna and Eleanor also engaged in long conversations, though striking quieter, more serious notes.

Mr. Repton's alterations and improvements, within doors and without, advance very properly. In blessing us with a mild winter, Mother Nature has proved a fine accomplice to our work. My involvement in the building plans is very small, and I am not at all ashamed to confess that, notwithstanding Mr. Repton's fine water-colour renderings, I am quite unable to speculate on the result of his proposal to extend a line on the Ground Plan by a half-inch here, or to add a second line there, necessitating the removal of a third. He is particularly opinionated about *prospects* and *aspects*. When the former conflicts with the latter, he exercises great ingenuity (he modestly assures his audience) in devising plans to satisfy their contradictory needs. He feels strongly that *aspect* (and you should know that a south-eastern aspect is preferred!) is far more important than *prospect*. Are you not diverted? He is often at odds with the sun itself when its daily journey does not take quite the direction to show Mr. Repton's work to full advantage. Were it in his power, I have no doubt that he would wish to "improve" the sun also. Nevertheless, I have every confidence that Mr. Darcy and Mr. Repton know what they are about, and limit my own opinions to wall-coverings and curtains, plants and shrubs. A border in the enlarged kitchen garden is being cleared to receive currants and gooseberry bushes, and a spot has been found proper for raspberries. We shall not attempt to vie with Weldon Abbey and The Great House for the finest strawberries, much to the disappointment of Hopwith, the head gardener, who harbours a not-so-secret ambition to outdo them both.

Not without a little trepidation, I informed Mr. Repton that I could not do without a syringa, for the sake of Cowper's line: "Laburnum rich in streaming gold; syringa, iv'ry pure." We talk also of a laburnum. Fortified by his approbation, I further summoned my courage to object to the narrowness of the path which Mr. Repton's plantation has left in one part of the rookery. He has since examined it himself, acknowledges it to be much too narrow, and promises to have it altered. Such are your Niece's contributions to posterity!

It has struck ten; I must go to breakfast where I hope to have the pleasure of my Husband's company if he is returned from shooting. Yesterday, accompanied by Mr.

Daley, he went out very early and came home like a bad shot, for they had killed nothing at all.

Yrs very affectionately,

E. Darcy

PEMBERLEY

SATURDAY DAY, 22[d] JANUARY, 1814

ear Sir,

I am obliged to you for the samples for my sitting room, and for your valued advice. I am in agreement with your suggestion of the darker yellow silk brocade for the chairs, but my preference for the draperies is the lighter of the yellow, rather than the green. I understand your concern that the effect of too much yellow may not be entirely pleasing, but can assure you that I shall like it very well.

Mr. Darcy begs me to add that he leaves for Town on 4th April and will remain at Grosvenor Street for three weeks. He trusts it may be convenient for you to wait upon him there.

I remain, my dear Sir,

E. Darcy

Humphry Repton, Esq.
Sloane Street
London

Great House
Saturday, 12th March, 1814

My dear Aunt Gardiner,

My beloved Sister begs me to inform you immediately of the arrival of Frederick Charles yesterday evening at eleven o'clock. Your Great-Nephew has a fine set of lungs, which he used to full effect as he announced himself to the world. We have so much cause for thankfulness: Mother and Child both safe, and Jane's bodily suffering only slight. Mr. Bingley is as overjoyed as a new Papa ought to be, and the proud Grandmamma has declared young Frederick the handsomest, healthiest, lustiest Newborn there ever was. She insists that Charlotte's Robert is nothing compared to Jane's Frederick, and she will surely waste no time telling Lady Lucas as much upon her return to Longbourn.

I return to Pemberley in a week. I wish I could accompany Mr. Darcy to Town next month, but it cannot be helped. As penance for abandoning an adoring Wife, I am preparing a long list of commissions for him to undertake on my behalf.

You will perhaps be surprised to hear that my Mother received a letter last week from Lydia (addressed to her here at The Great House) in which she longs to see her Mamma, her Sisters and her expected Nephew or Niece. She entreats Mamma to intercede with her Sisters and begs an invitation for herself and her dear Wickham to visit us all. You will certainly not be surprised to learn that since they have recently moved into new lodgings, naturally incurring various, unspecified expenses, would Mamma kindly ask Lizzy to send money for their travel expenses? (Indeed, sending a carriage for them is strongly hinted at, a hint immediately ignored by the Bingleys and Darcys.)

Moreover, Lydia's travel dress is so out of style that she has taken the liberty of ordering a new one, and feeling certain that her Sisters would not wish to be shamed by her appearance, she suggests that Jane and I share the cost. Sly, clever Lydia! In approaching our Mother, rather than addressing herself to Jane and me directly, she well knows that she is unlikely to be denied, though they will have to content themselves with travelling post.

All may yet work out well. They arrive at The Great House seven days hence, then she is to come to Pemberley (to which my Husband agrees) after Mr. Darcy has left for Town. Even Lydia accepts that it is impossible for Mr. Wickham to be received at Pemberley under any circumstances, but she gives us to understand that he will be continuing to Bath alone, returning to The Great House after two or three weeks. They will then return to Newcastle together to rejoin his regiment.

My Mother was only prevented from immediately sending for Kitty and Mary "for the very great pleasure of having my Girls together again" by the reminder that her eldest Daughter is in childbed, that her second Daughter's confinement is imminent, and that her Husband would thus be left entirely alone at Longbourn. A tearful moment followed wherein Mamma related how lonely and unhappy she is at Longbourn with three Daughters gone. The remaining two give her no pleasure at all. I was tempted to recall that just two years ago she was unhappy at having *five* unmarried Daughters at home, but since such a recollection would have distressed her even more, I for once followed Jane's example and said nothing.

Be assured of the love and regard of your affectionate Niece,

PEMBERLEY
FRIDAY, 8th APRIL, 1814

My dear Husband,

How glad I am to know that you are safely arrived at Grosvenor Street and that your journey was without incident. It was my fervent hope that this fine spring weather would accompany you to Town and I am thankful that the roads were dry and sound.

Thank you, I can think of no further commissions to add to my list. I shall, however, expect you to lay in a stock of intelligence sufficient to amuse me for a twelvemonth. Of course, gleaning such gossip for your dear Wife will entail attending dinner parties, theatre parties and all other manner of diversions and entertainments, but I trust that sacrificing your own inclination to dine at home and spend a quiet evening with a book before a good fire will not cost you *too* dearly. Should such a price be too high, however, even for a much-loved Spouse, pray content yourself with your books and the occasional company of my Uncle and Aunt Gardiner and know that your Lizzy will love you not one jot less!

Jane writes that she continues to make a good recovery, that our Nephew and Godson gets on well, that Mr. Bingley beams with fatherly pride. My Mother returns to Longbourn tomorrow; Lydia comes here following breakfast at The Great House. Mr. Bingley has graciously offered his carriage for the journey despite my assurance that you had ordered a carriage to be sent from here, but he insists.

A short letter announcing Georgiana's safe arrival at Rosings came on Tuesday last. I have been in hopes of a longer letter arriving each day since, but it is probably too much to expect and yet another indication of how much I miss her. Indeed, Pemberley is far too quiet (notwithstanding Mr. Repton's labourers) and in truth, I am heartily sick of being so long separated from my Dearest Life—today being the sixth day that you are gone from home!

These three weeks will be the longest separation we ever yet endured, but I am resolved to meet this trial with cheerful resignation. All my happiness and satisfaction in life date from the day of our betrothal, but since joy and affliction are dispensed by the same divine providence, let us trust that good sense will direct me to submit to the one as well as the other. (I fear I lack the courage to express these sentiments aloud, only in a letter am I able to open my heart without embarrassment. Is this perhaps the meaning of the saying that true intimacy thrives on separation?)

Please accept the affectionate love of a heart not so tired as the right hand belonging to it, and know that you are always in the thoughts of your loving and devoted Wife,

PEMBERLEY

WEDNESDAY, 13th APRIL, 1814

My dear Georgiana,

Take heart! Your Brother is yet in Grosvenor Street but I feel confident he would wish me to tell you that your marriage to Colonel Fitzwilliam will be arranged and will take place according to *your* wishes. As your Aunt, Lady Catherine is naturally at liberty to make suggestions. Remember, however, that you are under *no obligation* to accept them. Do not distress yourself, my dear Sister. I know that it is against your (and the Colonel's) easy-going, sweet temperament to contradict or disappoint others, especially members of your own family, but in this particular circumstance you are both at liberty (indeed, I would go further and say you are *obliged*) to listen to your own hearts to avoid the even greater unhappiness of disappointing your own good selves.

With your permission, I will venture a suggestion of my own: Listen to Lady Catherine's instructions and orders, and thank her for her interest and concern without further comment or acceptance. Although my own acquaintance of your Aunt is limited, I feel certain this will suffice. Should she offer personally to see to it that such-and-such is done, I know your Brother would wish you to inform your Aunt that *he* is undertaking all arrangements for your nuptials, and that she should address herself to *him*. (As a self-acknowledged arbiter of good taste, it is strange, is it not, that Lady Catherine is not aware that the old fashion of festivity and publicity at weddings is quite gone by, and is universally condemned as showing the bad taste of former generations, but pray do not mention it.) Above all, do all in your power to keep up your spirits, my dear Georgiana, for the want of spirits is the greatest misery.

Thank you, I am in good health. Thank you, too, for your compliments to my Sister, Lydia. Be assured that Jane and her little one do very well. Young Frederick repays the affection and love constantly showered upon him with smiles and a variety of delightful gurgles. I beg you will convey my respects to Lady Catherine, my regards to Colonel Fitzwilliam, and know that I am always your loving Sister,

Elizabeth

PEMBERLEY
SATURDAY, 16th APRIL, 1814

My dear Aunt Gardiner,

How glad I am to have the very real excuse of wanting to thank you promptly for your most welcome letter, thus allowing me to withdraw to the peace of my own room with a clear conscience on this rainy morning. Lydia declares herself bored (not for the first time since she arrived here). My suggestions that she read a book from the library, re-acquaint herself with the piano in the music room, or take up some needlework from the poor-basket (since she had brought none of her own) meet with vacant stares and a toss of the head. She spends her time walking about the house and banging doors, or ringing the bell for a glass of water.

I had earlier written suggesting she might want to bring books and needlework to Pemberley, which prompted the following reply: "You distress me cruelly by your request, Lizzy. I cannot think of any books to bring with me, nor have I any idea of needing them. I come to you to be talked to, not read to, or to hear reading. I can do *that* at home!"

Married life has changed my Sister but little. The pretty, empty-headed, vain girl is a little older, but marriage has not made her any more mature or sensible: that lively personality, which was found so engaging by many, is now tempered by an unpleasing air of discontent. There is not a conversation to be had in which she does not relate how she and her dear Wickham have been ill-used by the world, how unlucky they are, how unfair everyone is. I regret to say she does not confine such thoughts to private conversations when we are alone. It is fortunate that our acquaintance is too well-mannered to betray any surprise at her indiscretions, and the servants pretend not to hear, but I feel all the embarrassment of her loose tongue.

Mr. Darcy assures me that with Wickham an officer with the regulars, their income ought to be sufficient for them to live as they please if they are careful. Of course, they seldom are. As might be expected, Mr. Wickham is as full of easy charm and compliments as ever. All that was uncomfortable in our first meeting at The Great House soon passed away, leaving only the interesting charm of remembering former Meryton acquaintances. He departed for Bath much sooner than planned, staying at The Great House barely one week. Thus, he remains in Bath with a party of fellow officers an entire month. Lydia professes not to mind, indeed, one might almost imagine that she encouraged his change of plan. She assures us that her dear Wickham is in great need of rest and that the change of scene and the air at Bath will do him a power of good. She also hinted that perhaps his luck at the gaming tables might change for the better. His *adieux* were not long; and they would have been yet shorter, had he not been frequently detained by the urgent entreaties of his fair one that he should go. At length, however, he drew on his gloves with leisurely care and set off with a happy air of real conceit and affected indifference.

I need hardly mention that Georgiana was not of the party which welcomed the Wickhams at The Great House. Indeed, she and Colonel Fitzwilliam have been at Rosings for two weeks and will stay a fortnight longer. It will be in her power to bring me first-hand news of Charlotte, whom she visits often, no doubt in order to escape Lady Catherine, who has been issuing instructions as to the only suitable arrangements to be made for

Georgiana's marriage in November. Not surprisingly, Georgiana desires the simplest, quietest of ceremonies. Lady Catherine, feeling all the importance of Miss Darcy, daughter of Lady Anne, marrying the youngest son of an Earl, has a very different occasion in mind. In taking this strong, personal interest in Georgiana's nuptials, we must assume that Lady Catherine in fact intends to witness them. (Upon Georgiana's betrothal, my Husband wrote his Aunt a most conciliatory letter, to which he has yet to receive the honour of a reply.)

I should have mentioned this earlier (forgive me) but pray, do not fret that you will not be at my side while I am in child-bed. I, too, had presumed my Mother intended to remain with me at Pemberley where, incidentally, she could have prolonged her pleasure in Lydia's company by another fortnight. Yet Mama professed an urgent need—indeed, it was her duty—to return to Longbourn and my Father, having been absent far too long. I cannot help wondering whether other reasons persuaded her to return so urgently: my Mother continues to feel herself intimidated by Mr. Darcy, and to stay under his roof for several weeks without the support of Jane or Kitty, or even my Father, was an intolerable prospect. But I beg you not to concern yourself, my dear Aunt. I am in good health and spirits, though it would hardly be truthful if I said I was without anxiety or fear. However, I have faith that all will turn out well. One knows, of course, the uncertainty of all this, but we must think the best and hope the best.

We left Jane last Saturday in good spirits and restored health. It gives me such pleasure to see her and Mr. Bingley so happy. Frederick Charles is a strong infant with (as I mentioned previously) such a fine set of lungs, it is hard to believe he is the offspring of such soft-spoken parents. I confess to feeling a little envious and pray that Mr. Darcy and I will be as fortunate as the Bingleys.

A letter from Kitty just now arrived: Mamma is safely at Longbourn, but the journey has left her nerves in a poor state. My Mother remains exhausted following her anxiety over Jane's confinement and is urging Papa to take her to the seaside for several weeks at the very least this summer if he wishes to see her restored to her former self. She gave him to understand that, but for her very real concern for her Husband's health and happiness, she would—indeed, should—have stayed until Lizzy's confinement—yet her duty to her Husband outweighed every other concern, even a Mother's natural wish to be at her Daughter's side. Kitty adds that my Father was unmoved by this rare outpouring of spousal affection, and retired to his library forthwith. It is fortunate that my Mother's indifferent health did not prevent her calling upon Lady Lucas immediately following some restorative refreshment urged on her by Hill. Poor Kitty! Jane and I are resolved to have her with us as often as our Mother can do without her. It is too bad that she must be at my Mother's beck and call in the absence of any other diversions.

You cannot write too often. Bless you.

PEMBERLEY

TUESDAY, 19th APRIL, 1814

My dear Jane,

At last, a moment to myself! Lydia is gone into Lambton, which hitherto she had found "an excessively tedious place, with little in the way of fashion or style to recommend it," yet since my offer to purchase for her a prettily trimmed spring bonnet at Weaver's—by good fortune the exact colour of her new travelling dress—Lambton has gained a little in her favour. The village is, no doubt, grateful for the compliment.

I fear that our quiet life at Pemberley has disappointed our youngest Sister. Anna and Fanny Norland have been kind enough to wait upon us twice, for which I am indebted to them. They have little in common with Lydia, who made no effort to hide her boredom once she discovered they had little knowledge of, or interest in the latest fashion in hair ornaments and shoe trimmings. Sir Richard Mansfield who, as you know, needs little excuse for a party, generously gave a small one in Lydia's honour, but an absence of sufficient young men to dance and flirt with at Hurstbourne Park prevented the occasion being at all amusing, she informed me upon her return.

Mr. Darcy's business keeps him in town another fortnight. His hope that the matters which brought him there might be more speedily concluded was, sadly, a false one. I long for his return, and feel his absence keenly. His letters indicate that he is as anxious to be home again as I am to have him by my side. "As I look about me in fashionable company in London," he writes, "I see none I like half so much as my own dear Wife. Indeed, to enjoy the repose of my own fireside listening to my Wife, in her chair opposite, read a poem aloud, is my dearest wish." Is that not a sweet sentiment?

Notwithstanding my efforts to entertain our Sister, I spend my days in quiet and ease, exactly as you required of me. Profitably, too, for the basket at my side is nicely filled with nursery items, as is the poor-basket. How fortunate that I had few expectations of our Sister's needle making any contribution, else I should be sorely disappointed.

While I stitch, Mrs. Wickham leafs through copies of *La Belle Assemblée* and *Ackerman's Repository*, bemoaning all the while the unfairness of not being able to have all the gowns and bonnets to which she takes a fancy, and to which she feels entitled. I have chosen to ignore her hint that Mr. Wickham really ought to have a fancy toothpick case and that since Mr. Darcy is in town, might he not be persuaded to purchase one from Gray's?

How pleased I am to know that you and my Nephew continue in good health! And how dearly I wish I were able to travel with Lydia on the 24th to see you! However, since by way of compensation my dear Husband returns from town the following day, and with Georgiana rejoining us but three days later, pray do not feel *too* sorry for your devoted Sister,

PEMBERLEY

THURSDAY, 19th MAY, 1814

My dear Charlotte,

How quickly a year passes! It seems hardly possible that young Robert celebrates his first birthday next week. I rejoice that he is in excellent health and brings you such happiness, and can well imagine how proud Mr. Collins must be of such a fine son.

Immediately upon her return from Rosings, I uncharitably questioned Georgiana minutely and at great length about *you* and *your* family, when all the while poor Georgiana was longing for me to commiserate with *her* on her uncomfortable stay there. (By the bye, I am obliged to you for receiving G. so often and in such Sisterly fashion. She tells me that your kindness made the difficult audiences at Rosings much easier to bear, the more so because of your tact in *not* plying her with questions she may have found awkward to answer.)

You know, perhaps, that Lady Catherine was on the point of taking over the wedding arrangements herself, thus obliging Georgiana and the Colonel to inform their Aunt of their own wish for a simple, quiet ceremony; that while they were both loath to disappoint their Aunt, in this instance, however, &c., &c.

Lady Catherine, not a woman to be gainsaid, did not receive this well-intentioned speech well. It is a tribute to the good natures and temperaments of both that they bore the frankness of her Ladyship's remarks so valiantly. Knowing them both so well, it must have pained them exceedingly to have gone against her wishes; only their greater fear of the outcome were Lady C. to have her way armed them for the fray. (I relate the above at Georgiana's request. She is exceedingly thankful to you, feeling most uncomfortable and ungrateful that she was obliged to be so secretive at the time. Having reassured her that you were to be trusted not to reveal any confidences she might share with you, she begged me to tell you all and extends heartfelt apologies for her earlier wariness.)

You may not yet have heard—since the letter only arrived a few days ago—that Colonel Fitzwilliam's Father is to give them a fine house on his estate. They are both most deserving of his generosity and I am delighted for them, but I shall miss Georgiana dreadfully. We have known each other but a short time, yet I am as fond of her as a Sister could be, and (dare I say it?) take a little credit for her blossoming into a fine young woman with a little *more* confidence and a great deal *less* fear of the world than when we first met. Since I am boasting, let me also take a little more credit for her changing relationship with her Brother, who previously (because of their difference in age and the early death of their Father) was more Father figure than Brother. I now take great delight in observing them in conversation: occasionally, she will make so bold as to actually contradict him, or even offer an opinion of her own! I hasten to add that an exchange such as this only takes place in the intimacy of our Family circle—she is not yet brave enough to venture a contradictory opinion in company. Since her betrothal to Colonel Fitzwilliam, of course, she has blossomed even further, and it gives us both much joy to see her at last happy and contented. It will be an excellent match with great affection on both sides.

Dear Charlotte, let me once again thank you for your many kindnesses to Georgiana. Friendship is indeed a precious gift, of more real value than the finest gold. Be assured that I treasure ours.

Affectionately,
Elizabeth

PEMBERLEY
MONDAY, 13th JUNE, 1814

My dear Aunt Gardiner,

You will by now have received Mr. Darcy's express informing you of the arrival of Anne Elizabeth on the 7th. He will not, however, have praised her sufficiently so I hasten to inform you of her particulars. Thankfully, she has the usual number of arms, legs, fingers and toes, but there her similarity with any other Infant ends. From her full head of soft, brown curls, to her large brown eyes fringed with long dark eyelashes, down to her tiny feet she is perfection. Were Shakespeare alive, I feel confident the mere sight of her would inspire a sonnet or two. But I am remiss in forgetting to describe the smile which lights up her dear, sweet face, and which clearly indicates her joy at finding herself in the world.

(I fear little Annie may succeed in turning her Mamma into another Lady Mansfield, boring the world with the wonders of her Child, the likes of which it has never seen.)

It is my decided opinion that Annie bears every likeness to her Papa. Her Papa disagrees, insisting that her fine brown eyes and brown curls are her Mamma's alone. You shall decide the matter when you are next at Pemberley. My Husband's delight in the birth of his Daughter almost exceeds my own. My love for him, the Father of my Child, grows in strength, and I look upon myself as the happiest of women. Not a day passes that I do not give thanks for my many blessings and good fortune.

At Matins yesterday, my Husband was touched by the generosity and sincerity of the many good wishes and congratulations offered him. He had ordered the church bells rung once it was certain that Wife and Daughter were safely delivered, and instructed Mrs. Reynolds to arrange a celebration for the servants that they might share our joy.

One of life's blessings is that Lady Catherine lives at a sufficient distance to necessitate the communication of her lengthy advice by letter. Poor Charlotte, how can she bear to have every aspect of her family life dictated and overseen by such a person? Yet I remind myself that Charlotte is of quite a different sort of temperament from myself and well able to handle Lady Catherine in her own quiet fashion. I think it will be best not to reply to her instructions on the selection and hiring of wet-nurses, a subject requiring two full pages of her Ladyship's fine notepaper to fully describe. As it is, I have no intention whatever of employing a wet-nurse and intend to suckle my Child myself. It is the modern way and while I am no creature of fashion, in this case, fashion corresponds precisely with my own opinion. I shall not be one of those Mothers who consign their Children to the nursery and to the care of a governess, to be paraded in the drawing room when convenient. No, I shall not become a stranger to my Children. Indeed, my dear Aunt, as a Mother my dearest wish is to have as close and loving and a relationship with my Children as you and my Uncle have with yours. I shall look to you for guidance and advice.

The weather does not know how to be otherwise than fine. The Daleys sent over a fine basket of strawberries this morning with which we shall probably make jam, for Jane brought a goodly quantity from her own beds. (Dear Jane, bless her. She was such a strength to me during my Daughter's birth, I know not how I should have got on without her. She remains here another three days.)

Affectionately,

E.D.

P.S. Mr. Darcy tells me of your invaluable assistance in selecting the string of pearls from Gray's. It is perfect in every way and will always be a treasured reminder (in the unlikely event that I shall ever be in need of one) of my Daughter's birth, the love of my Husband and the affections of a cherished Aunt.

PEMBERLEY
TUESDAY, 14th JUNE, 1814

My dear Mamma,

Your letter arrived this morning and finds us all in good health. Let me assure you that Mr. Darcy is by no means disappointed with his Daughter; quite the contrary, he is delighted with her. There is no cause for distress, and I entreat you to cease your concern that your Grandchild is not a boy. We are thankful that Annie is healthy and strong; she already brings us great happiness and you will afford me a great honour by sharing in it.

Jane returns to The Great House on Thursday. Mr. Bingley does not merely send the carriage for her, but comes himself with Frederick Charles and the Nurse—a first meeting for the two Cousins.

My Sister begs me send her love to you and to our Father, to which I add my own.

PEMBERLEY

SATURDAY, 18th JUNE, 1814

Dear Lady Catherine,

Thank you for your kind congratulations on the birth of our Daughter. Indeed, you are correct: her name honours the memory of your Sister, Mr. Darcy's Mother, and I trust she will prove herself worthy of it in the years to come.

I am also deeply obliged to you for your words of advice; it was most kind of you to take so much of your valuable time to impart your own experience, and I intend to make careful study of your words, particularly since you mention that my dear friend, Mrs. Collins (whose good sense I value highly) has benefited so greatly from them. Your Ladyship may rest assured that I am resolved to be a good Mother to my Children, to pray for them, to set them good examples, to give them good advice, to be careful both of their souls and bodies, and to watch over their tender minds. Since (as you say) my Children will have all the advantage of wealth and position, I am sure you will agree that as their Parents, Mr. Darcy and I will be obliged to remind them how privileged they are, and instill in them the qualities of good character, modesty, integrity and compassion for others, without which wealth and position are meaningless.

In closing, I should like to add my own wish to Mr. Darcy's that you will consent to attend the nuptials of Georgiana and Colonel Fitzwilliam in November, and do us the further honour of staying at Pemberley. This will also afford you the opportunity to see Mr. Repton's work for yourself and, I trust, be reassured that his alterations have done nothing but enhance Pemberley's beauty. (My Husband begs me add that, as you had requested, Georgiana did indeed report your opinion of Mr. Repton to him. He is much obliged.) Mr. Darcy joins me in the hope that your Daughter's health will allow her to accompany you here.

Ever yours,

E. Darcy

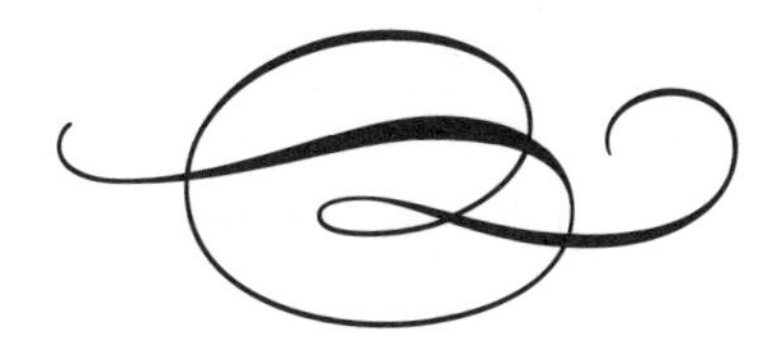

Pemberley
Monday, 20th June, 1814

My dear Lady Mansfield,

Knowing how little you like being away from home and your Children, the honour of your call was most deeply appreciated. Your devotion to your Children is indeed exemplary and much remarked upon among our acquaintance as the finest example of Motherhood, and a standard to which we should all aspire.

Your advice did not fall upon deaf ears, I assure you, and it was especially pleasing to know that we share similar views on so many topics. That we should disagree on a few trifling points is therefore of little import and I would not wish you to consider any differing views of mine as any criticism of yours. My choosing not to employ a wet-nurse, against your advice, may or may not be a modern fad, but in nursing my Child myself, I am obeying my instincts as a Mother, selfish instincts I have simply chosen not to deny.

On the subject of obedience and discipline in Children, I entirely agree that they are indispensable in their upbringing. All I intended to imply was that perhaps it is imprudent to call them forth *too* frequently on trivial occasions. Fear and force will, of course, govern Children when small, but I feel certain that having a strong hold on their *affections* will have the most influence over them as they journey through Life.

In saying thus much, I was speaking in the most general of terms, and certainly not passing comment on you, dear Lady Mansfield. From my own observation, your Children are exceedingly well-behaved and their devotion to their Mother boundless.

If my words caused you offence, I apologise unreservedly and beg forgiveness. Any offence was quite unintended, I assure you. I hope I may be permitted to seek your valuable advice in future—I know I shall be in need of it—and also know that there is nobody of my acquaintance so experienced and dedicated to the proper care of their Children as you.

Yours faithfully,

Elizabeth Darcy

PEMBERLEY

TUESDAY, 16th AUGUST, 1814

You are too kind, my dear Aunt. To take it upon yourself to assist Georgiana in the purchase of wedding clothes is more than generous. I must include my Uncle, too, for his own generosity in sparing you for this undertaking.

To own the truth, we were all mightily relieved to have your offer: Miss Bingley wrote a long letter of congratulation on Annie's birth, adding that since I would be unable to accompany Georgiana to town for wedding clothes, and knowing that she (Miss B.) would be more likely than I to know the best shops, she would willingly cut short her stay with friends in Sussex to put herself at G.'s disposal. Until that moment, while we might well have given a passing thought to wedding clothes, it was ever a subject for later discussion and consequently dismissed from our minds. A birth, an Infant and latterly a christening have filled our days, and now the calendar informs us that later is now! Thank you again, dear Aunt, for your forethought. For her part, Georgiana did not wish to put herself forward lest she should appear avaricious. Silly goose!

As you might expect, Mr. Darcy has made a most generous allowance for wedding clothes, so there is no need for either you or Georgiana to concern yourselves on that score. G. and I have begun a list of commissions: shoes, stockings, gloves, hats, feathers and trimmings, morning and visiting dresses, cloaks, shawls, wraps, riding habits, ball gowns. (The mantua-maker here makes her wedding gown, but Georgiana will need to purchase ivory buttons for it from William & Son.) Should this long list alarm you, dear Aunt, you are, of course, at liberty to amend it as you see fit, and as your time and energy allow.

A commission from Mr. Darcy, if you please: He requests, nay insists, that you both pay a visit to Bourgeois Amick & Sons in the Haymarket. There, you and Georgiana are to purchase the finest scent of your choice with his best compliments. (I am also to add that arrangements have already been made for these items to be charged to Mr. D.'s account.)

I blush at my own impudence, yet cannot resist asking that *if* you should pass by Lackington's, would you purchase a copy of a new Scottish novel, *Waverley*, for me? The author remains anonymous, but by all accounts it is a great success. Lady Ashton Dennis tells me that Byron's *Lara* is to be published this month and I should dearly love a copy if it does not put you to too much trouble.

How dearly I wish that I, too, could be of the party. What a merry time we would have, the three of us. Instead, Georgiana has been charged to write me daily of your doings; I want to know every particular so that I may be properly envious!

I shall now write Miss Bingley that she should remain happily in Sussex.

With my best love, as always,

PEMBERLEY
MONDAY, 14th NOVEMBER, 1814

My dear Aunt,

I have had not a moment's time to write, or you should not have been left so long in ignorance of all the particulars of Georgiana's wedding to Colonel Fitzwilliam. I hasten to make amends.

The day dawned clear and temperate; the bride and groom were as nervous as they ought to be; the bride's handsome Brother was by turns bursting with pride and deeply affected by the honour of giving his only Sister in marriage to his Cousin and dear friend. The bride's dress was of snow-white muslin, and over it a fine silk shawl, white, shot with primrose, and all over embossed with white satin flowers. The delicate yellow tints were most becoming to her fair hair and sunny, clear complexion, though her natural sweet modesty was the most graceful ornament to her beauty.

Dear Georgiana, in never seeking admiration, she will always find it. Some lines of George Crabbe came to me as I observed her:

Her air, her manners, all who saw admir'd;
Courteous though coy, and gentle though retired
The joy of youth and health her eyes displayed,
And ease of heart her every look conveyed.

I ought to say something about the bridegroom, though he is but a secondary figure on these occasions and rarely mentioned in reports of weddings. But since he plays an important role in the proceedings, I shall give him his due and tell you that the Colonel cut a very fine figure indeed in his dress uniform.

Lady Catherine and Miss de Bourgh honoured us with their presence, arriving at Pemberley (unannounced) just three days before. Knowing that they planned to attend—Lady C. finally having informed my Husband of her intention—I had had rooms prepared three weeks prior and aired daily since. Mr. Darcy and I had anyhow resolved not to be put out by anything her Ladyship might say or do, so it was of little matter. She lost little time in inspecting Mr. Repton's alterations and additions, opined that I should regret the particular shade of yellow chosen for my sitting room draperies—they will quickly fade—and declared the new servants' wing an error in judgment and taste. The new conservatory left her quite speechless, I am told, a rare event I am sorry not to have witnessed. Thankfully, she stopped short of declaring Pemberley "ruined," yet that was the unspoken sentiment. My Husband, I am proud to say, while tested beyond the limits of endurance by Lady C.'s lectures on good taste and style, exercised great forbearance and restraint. Towards myself, Lady Catherine was as polite as good manners dictated and I am indebted to her for choosing to ignore me for the most part.

Your Great-Niece, subjected to similar close inspection was, regrettably, found much wanting in disposition. Her merry eyes and ready smiles are evidently not desirable traits in an Infant of five months, and prompted her Ladyship to remark, that "All Children are by nature evil, Mrs. Darcy. Prudent parents must check their naughty passions in any way they have in their power and force them into decent and proper behaviour." My poor, poor Charlotte! How she must daily suffer! Our Daughter's failings notwithstanding, Lady Catherine did deem her fit to receive a very fine brooch with which to mark her birth.

You will recall that Lady Catherine had very decided ideas about her Niece's nuptials. It was hardly surprising, therefore, that she was overheard to declare the occasion a "very dull affair: very little white satin, very few lace veils; a most pitiful business," yet I can assure you that for all other parties concerned, who do not share her Ladyship's taste for finery and parade, the simplicity of the nuptials added a real elegance to the occasion.

I had, at last, the opportunity to meet Colonel Fitzwilliam's Father and found him a fine, genial man of good sense, not at all like his Sister, Lady Catherine (to whom he paid scant attention). Mr. Darcy remembers him and his Mother, Lady Anne, being much alike in temperament, favouring their own Father in disposition.

As a special surprise, Mr. Darcy arranged for Mrs. Annesley (G.'s former companion) to attend the wedding—my Husband's thoughtfulness never ceases to astonish me, and in this instance he was well rewarded by the warmth of their embraces and their obvious affection for one another. Many tenants, villagers, farm workers and others crowded outside the church for a glimpse of the bride, shouting blessings and good wishes, and Mr. Darcy made sure that everyone at Pemberley could celebrate the occasion in style by arranging festivities in the new servants' wing, complete with music for dancing.

The newly-weds prudently decided to postpone a wedding journey to the Continent. While Napoleon is safely imprisoned at Elba for the moment, rumours abound that he has plans to escape. Moreover, the Colonel would not wish to be far from his regiment in these uncertain times. So they are spending their first weeks as Man and Wife in their new house, happily engaged in domestic rather than cultural pursuits.

Now we find ourselves quite alone again, but by no means repining (though, of course, Georgiana is sorely missed). We shall join the Bingleys for the Christmas festivities. Mr. Darcy keenly looks forward to good sport; Jane and I will be perfectly satisfied with our own company and Children. I shall endeavour not to mind *too* greatly the want of a favourite Aunt to complete our party, and content myself with the happy thought that we shall see each other in London in the New Year. Meanwhile, let me thank you again for your part in making the occasion of Georgiana's wedding such a joyous one for all of us. Your absence was keenly felt by many, not least by your devoted Niece,

1815

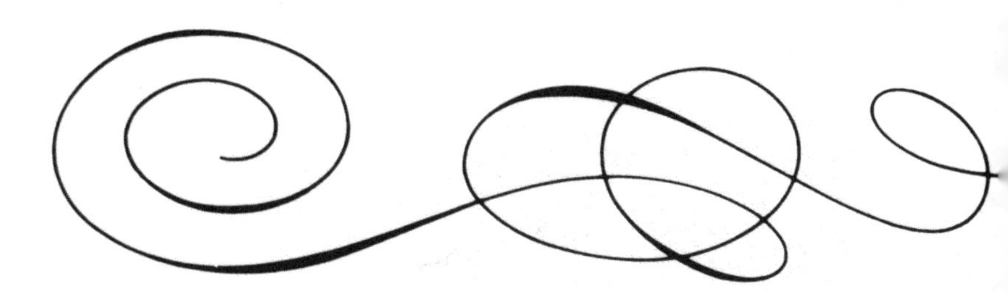

GROSVENOR STREET, LONDON
MONDAY, 23rd JANUARY, 1815

My dear Jane,

I should have written long before and beg forgiveness for causing you such concern. We are safely arrived in London following an arduous journey (from which I hasten to assure you we are all now fully recovered.) With many apologies for my shameful neglect (and in part to excuse it) let me lay before you the particulars of our journey here, although there are parts which I would prefer to forget entirely. In saying thus much, I know I may rely on your confidentiality; indeed, I would prefer even Mr. Bingley not to be apprised of *every* detail, but must leave that to your discretion, which I trust implicitly.

Our first day from Pemberley, the weather was fair and dry and remained so the entire way to Longbourn, which we reached in excellent time. We stayed but two nights and set out for London early on the 7th. We were not on the road long before the sky darkened and snow began to fall, lightly at first, then the wind gusted in an instant, turning pretty flakes into a blinding storm of whirling snow. Mr. Darcy, whose mood had darkened with the weather, instructed Thompson to stop at the next inn where we would wait until the storm abated. Not five minutes later we heard a loud crack and were pitched over into a ditch! Having first ensured that we were all unhurt, Mr. Darcy and Thompson unhitched the horses which were frightened but otherwise unscathed, thankfully. The horses were then hitched behind the second carriage in some fashion and we set out again to find an inn and send help and fresh horses back to Thompson, who was left to guard our carriage. Annie, who was with Nurse in the second carriage, slept through the whole commotion, bless her heart, and the only sounds to be heard were the muffled steps of the horses. Mr. Darcy was by now in the blackest of moods and I was glad to finally hear that young Thompson (Thompson's son) saw lights ahead. Never was I so pleased to see a warm fire!

Once he had arranged rooms and ordered dinner for us all, Mr. Darcy went with young Thompson to settle the horses and make arrangements with the landlord to collect Thompson, our belongings, and have the carriage repaired. Our own valises being still with the carriage, I had nothing to do but see that Nurse and Annie were comfortable, and rest until Mr. Darcy returned. I was rudely awakened by the loud slamming of a door to see Mr. Darcy standing before me.

"Mrs. Darcy," he railed, "I do hope you are well aware that none of this would have happened if I had not been so foolish as to acquiesce to *your* insistence that we travel to London now rather than wait until late March as had been *my* wish. Also against my wishes, *you* insisted on our Daughter accompanying us—imagine if *she* had been in the carriage that overturned! Now here we are—heaven alone knows where—and heaven alone knows how long we may be stranded in this, this . . . place!

"And while you have been resting comfortably, I wonder if you have considered the welfare of the horses, the expense and time which will be incurred to repair the carriage? It is insupportable, Madam! In indulging your whims, I find myself in the abhorrent position of depending on persons completely unknown to me to rescue my family and servants from an unnecessary predicament which could, indeed, should have been avoided."

Before I had a chance to reply (though I was so shocked at this outburst as to be rendered quite speechless) he turned on his heel and quitted the room. Jane, I knew not what to think. These were the harshest words I had ever heard from his lips and for a moment wondered if I had awoken from a bad dream.

How long I sat there, I know not. Mr. Darcy's words rang in my head over and over again. I revisited conversations we had had previously about travelling at this time. Yes, he had wanted to leave later, but agreed with me that we should not deprive my Mother sight of her Granddaughter for too much longer, adding that travel can be just as hazardous in March with muddy, slippery roads. So it was that we spent the Christmas festivities at Longbourn. Much as I tried, I could not recollect a single instance of my insisting on anything with which I had been charged. Was I deceiving myself? Had I abused his kind, generous nature to such base purpose so often that he finally lost control of his temper? What had I done and how was I to make amends? My attempts to solve the conundrum succeeded only in bringing on a severe headache, yet somehow I managed to tidy myself, dress for dinner and attend to Annie's needs, the while hoping my demeanour might deceive the Nurse into thinking that nothing was amiss, though it was difficult to imagine that she had not heard at least part of Mr. Darcy's invective.

It was now time for dinner and I descended the stairs with some trepidation. Willpower alone permitted me to keep my composure as the landlord presented Mr. Darcy's apologies for his absence.

"'E insisted on goin' back out with the men, Ma'am. Said 'e 'ad t'be sure 'is man was safe. Said for me t'pack up food'n drink for all and to stop 'ere and look after 'is fam'ly and 'orses, Ma'am. I told 'im 'tweren't right a Gentleman like 'im goin' out in a storm like this, but 'e insisted, Ma'am. A right fine Gentleman that, Ma'am, if yer don't mind me sayin' so."

With that, he escorted me to the table where I was to dine alone. I may have graced the table with my presence, but my appetite had long taken flight. Nevertheless, so as not to appear ungracious, I did my best to eat the substantial meal set before me and drank a little wine to steady my nerves for I knew not what was yet to come. A brisk walk after dinner would have been just the thing, but snow was still falling steadily, so I retired instead to my chamber with a book, fooling myself that I might actually read! Perhaps it was the wine, perhaps the exertions of the day, but I fell asleep. When I finally awoke, it took a little time to recall where I was, then the day's events slowly seeped into my consciousness as my heart slowly sank with the remembrance.

"Are the men yet safely returned, Landlord?" I enquired.

"Not yet, Ma'am," said he, "but don't 'e worry. They'll be along presently, I reckons. The snow stopped about an hour ago and the sky's clearing nicely."

And so it was, with more and more stars to be seen as the clouds gradually cleared and the moon shone forth on the white landscape. Had my heart not been so heavy, it would have been a wondrous night, the sort of night my Husband and I had often enjoyed together at Pemberley, our arms wrapped around each other against the cold air. Jane, you can imagine that my spirits were at a very low ebb as I made my way back to my chamber. I lay in bed listening for sounds of his return, not expecting to sleep, but the next I knew it was morning and a maid arrived with hot water. "Mornin', Ma'am," she greeted me.

"Tell me, did the rescue party return? Is everyone safe?" I asked.

"Aye, Ma'am. They're all safe and sound, God be praised. 'Twas late by the time they got back 'ere, mind. An' now the snow's stopped, the wheelwright and 'is men'll be able to fix up your carriage in no time, I'll be bound."

She turned to leave, then turned back. "Silly me, I almost forgot. Yer 'usband said to give 'ee this as soon as you was awake," and handed me a letter. "Oh, and, if you please, Ma'am, the Gent'man says to send word when it'll be convenient for 'im to come up."

After she left, I looked at the letter several times wondering at its contents and, fearing a continuation of his last outburst, took a deep breath, tore it open and read (Jane, I beg you, at the very least, please keep this part to yourself):

"Elizabeth, my dearest Wife, can you ever forgive me for such ill-mannered behaviour? My outburst was so out of character—I hope we may agree on that—that I frightened myself exceedingly. Heaven alone knows how it must have affected you! When the storm began, my only thought was of the hazards which might lie before us and how foolish I had been to endanger the lives of not only the two dearest people to me in the world, but also our servants and horses. As the carriage overturned, I imagined you crushed to death and our Daughter in the following carriage meeting a similar fate. Indeed, even though that carriage was unharmed, seeing her fast asleep–for that brief, horrible moment, I imagined her dead.

"It will not surprise me if you cannot believe that my fury was directed only at myself—not at you, nor as a consequence of any actions of yours. It is nevertheless the truth. After the calamitous events of the day, my increasing anxiety led to a spleen filled to overflowing and able to take no more—so it was vented on you, something for which I am utterly ashamed. How could I have wounded the most important and dearest treasure of my life? In hurting you, I have hurt myself one-hundred-fold, diminishing my entire being. My only excuse is that the vehemence of my anger was brought about by the unbearable notion of harming, or losing you and our Daughter through my own gross stupidity and lack of control over our circumstances. I hope you will find it in your heart, dearest Lizzy, to forgive your most abject and loving Husband."

Jane, can you possibly imagine my relief? As I was reading his letter a second time (or was it a third or fourth?) a knock at the door announced Mr. Darcy's arrival. There was no need for words: my smiling face, wet with tears, and outstretched arms told him he was heartily forgiven; the warmth and ardour of his loving embrace confirmed that we would be as before, 'tho perhaps a little wiser and more appreciative of the blessings we enjoy.

I shall dwell no more on this most unhappy episode, except to say that we were obliged to stay at the inn three full days before the carriage was ready. We took full advantage of this unexpected leisure and enjoyed many walks into the surrounding country, complimenting Mother Nature on her snowy beauty as we went, and thanking her for the brilliant sunshine which showed her to best advantage.

Dear Jane, I shall write again soon. Be assured that your commission for Mr. Steele's Lavender Water causes no inconvenience.

Affectionately,

Grosvenor Street, London
Monday, 20th February, 1815

Dearest Jane,

London is very drab indeed. All is grey and damp and foggy with not even the winter fair on the Thames to lift the spirits—for the first time anyone can recall, the river is not frozen over, but we find plenty to amuse ourselves. Last Thursday, being an unusually fine day, we took the opportunity for some fresh air and drove out to some nearby villages: Kensington, Chelsea and Knightsbridge, which reminded me how much I look forward to returning to our own countryside. That same evening, we visited the Vauxhall Gardens. I don't recall that you were ever there so I must describe them to you: they comprise a series of gravel walks lined with trees and shrubbery, some quite secluded with names such as Dark Walk and Lovers' Walk, and throughout waterfalls and caves and marble statues. A central square is surrounded by pavilions and rotundas, all dedicated to the arts, in addition to a sizeable concert hall and picture gallery. Most fascinating of all, though, is the lighting. Mr. Darcy had already told me of the new gas lighting, which he has in mind to install at Pemberley one day, and this was his main interest in coming to Vauxhall. Jane, you would not believe it—more than one thousand lamps, we are told, all concealed in the trees and reflected in revolving mirrors, as well as chandeliers and lanterns. It is an astonishing sight, which would require another entire page to describe, but I shall leave the rest for you to discover for yourself. The Prince Regent was not in attendance that evening, having entertained a large party there just two days prior, we were told. I was only a little disappointed at the news—a *very* little.

We dine with my Uncle and Aunt Gardiner again tomorrow, after which we go together to Covent Garden. My Aunt and I have made several shopping expeditions when the weather has permitted; when not, we are perfectly content to sit at home with our work, where we are also far better situated for my Aunt to admire her Great-niece. We have also been reading Byron's *Corsair* together, so you see how happily we get on.

Mr. Darcy has also been busily occupied, not only with business matters, but also visits to his tailor, Mr. Weston in Bond Street; his hatter at Lock's; and his wine merchant at Berry's. My Aunt and I vastly prefer to occupy ourselves at Gunter's in Berkeley Square (in our opinion the best confectioners in London). By the time I leave town, we hope to have sampled most of their delicious wares and I have in mind to bring a large box of our favourites for you to enjoy. I shall insist on them securing the box tightly with many complicated knots to prevent your Sister from the temptation of sampling the contents anew!

Ever yours,

PEMBERLEY
SUNDAY, 14th MAY, 1815

My dear Jane,

I have so many matters to discuss that my paper will hardly hold it all. Little matters they are to be sure, but highly important nonetheless.

A letter from Mr. Collins this morning that Charlotte is safely delivered of a Daughter, to be named Catherine Maria. Mr. Collins expounds at length on the civility and generosity of his patroness, to whom he applied for the honour of naming her thus. That Lady Catherine should permit *his* Daughter to bear *her* name is a compliment of the highest order, he continues, for which he and his dear Charlotte feel appropriately humble and grateful and privileged. (I dare say some practical benefits may also ensue, do you not think? Lady C. has further honoured the Collinses by allowing her sickly Daughter to be Godmother.) Poor little Catherine, with such a name she will have much to live up to. Better she should have been named for Charlotte, but she is at least blessed with a Mother of abundant good sense to guide her through the pitfalls that will surely await the namesake of Lady Catherine de Bourgh!

My second piece of news is that this coming December promises the arrival of a Sister or Brother for Annie! Mr. Darcy is overjoyed at the prospect of an addition to our family; I am overjoyed that thus far I am in good health with no sign of the dizziness and nausea that I well remember at this stage with Annie—in fact, should the weather remain fair this afternoon, I have in mind to gather cowslips. Their delicious scent is one of the greatest pleasures Nature has to bestow, and cowslip wine in winter is a fond remembrance of the joys of spring.

Lastly, Mrs. Reynolds, who was sorry to hear about your cook's ailing feet, begs me to write these recipes, which she assures me will give certain relief:

1. *To assuage the raging pain of a Corn by instant application.*
   Take equal parts of a roasted onion and soft soap, beat them up together, and apply them to the corn in a linen rag by way of a poultice.

2. *Corn Plaister*

Take one ounce of turpentine, half an ounce of red lead, one ounce of frankincense, half a pound of white rosin, one pint of Florence oil; boil these ingredients in a pipkin, and keep stirring them over a slow fire with an elder stick until it turns black; then turn it out to harden for use. It must be applied by spreading it on a piece of leather oiled all over, and then put to the corn. Wearing it constantly for some time will effectually eradicate the corn.

Do you recall Mrs. Hill concocting some similar potion when our Mother was so afflicted?

If Mr. Darcy were not presently discussing with Barford such pressing matters of business as the prices of wheat, barley and sheep, I know he would wish me to send his compliments.

My mention of Mr. Darcy's steward reminds me to tell you that I paid another visit to Mrs. Barford yesterday. It is now almost a full year that her youngest Child died, yet her grief consumes her still.

The boy was scarce three years, so she is fortunate in being unburdened by long *years* of happy memories of him, and has three other Children besides. I reminded her (kindly, I hope) that her good Husband has great need of her, as do the other Children, and she would do well to rouse herself on their account and set her sorrow aside. I have no doubt you would have put it better, but Barford is a good, hardworking man upon whom my Husband places great reliance. It pains me to see him looking so sad, and I feel certain that if his good Lady made an attempt to greet him with a smile when he returns home, he would reap the benefit of it.

And so, my dear Jane, another glorious day beckons. This dry, warm spell must be heaven-sent for your strawberries. May we expect a large crop this year?

With love,

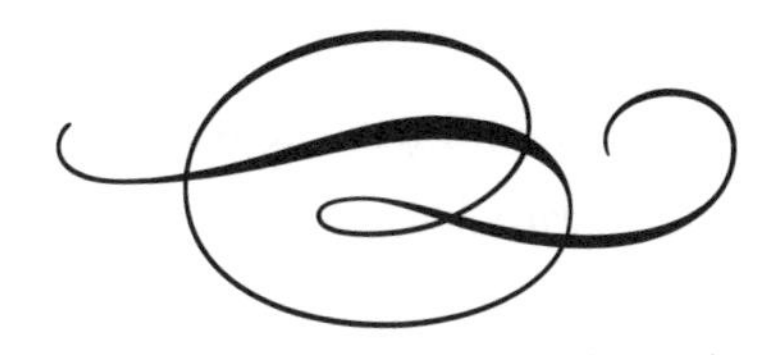

PEMBERLEY

TUESDAY, 10th OCTOBER, 1815

My dear, dear Eleanor,

You sly fox! I should scold you severely for having kept me in ignorance for so long about your sea captain, but I am too full of joy for you. My heartiest, sincerest congratulations on your betrothal. That your relationship has withstood the severe test of several years' separation is surely the best illustration of the steadfastness of your regard for one other and certainly an indication of loving and rewarding years ahead. I like your Captain already: to have waited for you for so long shows a steady, patient temperament and an appreciation of the treasure that is you, dear Eleanor. Mr. Darcy joins me in wishing you many years of happiness.

You only allude to the reasons for your former separation and, naturally, they are of no consequence now, yet my heart tells me that those years were surely not without great pain and suffering. Since I have had the pleasure of your acquaintance (may I say, friendship?) you have never once given any indication of the loneliness and sorrow you must surely have felt at times. How brave you have been, all the while keeping your own counsel, with not even a loving Sister to confide in! I have always held you in high esteem; my admiration for your fortitude and character is now boundless.

You also make passing mention of the jealousy of your Sister and the indifference of your Father, so I shall allow myself the presumption of saying that I feel certain you will rise above such pettiness, as you doubtless have had to do many times in the past. Let no feelings of hurt at their treatment of you be allowed to mar your joy! They who have contributed so little to your happiness in the past are hardly deserving of any consideration in your future.

No, I have not had news of Lady Ashton Dennis for some time. Now that she spends most of her time in Bath and moves in circles in which we have small or no acquaintance, we have too little in common to sustain a regular correspondence. One thing we do share is a love of good poetry, and now and then we exchange views on something or other we have lately read which the other might also enjoy. Her approval of your Betrothed can only add a measure to your joy and my own, since she is a woman of good taste and opinion.

How very fitting that just now your Captain has got the appointment which he has long been desirous of having! That you are to live on board ship is such an exciting prospect, my single regret being that we shall not see you and meet your Captain before you set sail for the Bahamas. Such an adventure for you! Shall you like being on the high seas? I questioned Mr. Darcy on the wisdom of setting sail at this time of year. He assures me that as your voyage progresses, you will be sailing towards very fair weather and will likely escape winter entirely—what joy! I have since found the Bahamas on the globe–such a long, long way from Bath! Pray, write often about life aboard ship and in the tropics. Your friend in land-locked Derbyshire looks forward to your reports with the greatest interest. Please know that our good wishes go with you.

As ever,
E.D.

PEMBERLEY

WEDNESDAY, 25th OCTOBER, 1815

A hasty note, my dear Jane, to accompany these apples. Mr. Darcy is sending Barford on business which will bring him within five miles of The Great House, and this season's apple crop is so bountiful that we are glad of the opportunity to share a bushel or two with you, knowing that your own orchards are yet too young to provide much fruit.

Life at Pemberley and the home farm has been busy of late: I am also sending you two flitches of ham and some newly-bottled gooseberries and damsons. Poor Barford must sorely regret my having overheard him talking to my Husband about his journey, for he is also making a similar delivery to Mrs. Harville (a former schoolfellow of Aunt

Gardiner's whose acquaintance I first made when we drove that first time to The Great House on your behalf—Mrs. H. resides in one of the villages along the way, the name of which I forget and must find before Barford sets out. Perhaps you have already met her?)

I hope these lines find you in good health and spirits, and that Frederick is quite recovered from his cold. I shall close now and scribble a note to Mrs. Harville.

Ever yours,
E.D.

1816

PEMBERLEY

FRIDAY, 12th JANUARY, 1816

I am heartily ashamed of myself, my dear Charlotte, that it has taken me so long to thank you for your good wishes on the birth of Cassandra Jane, who in four days will be four weeks old. I could offer the excuse that my recovery from child-bed has been slow, that I have been left weak and listless, but you will remember how much pride I take in my honesty and forthrightness (not always to my credit, let it be said) so I must tell you immediately that I am well-recovered, in good health and heart, and that my Daughter thrives. Let me also admit that my neglect of a favourite correspondent is due entirely to an indulgence in the happy state in which I find myself. Indeed, against custom and advice, I insisted upon leaving my bed after only one week, despite the entreaties of Mr. Brownley, abetted by my Husband. The prospect of spending another week abed when I felt so well was too hard to bear.

Annie is quite delighted with her Sister, though persists in calling her Rosebud, the name of her favourite doll. Cassie appears to consider this a great compliment and has made no objection thus far. Indeed, Cassie does resemble a doll, a tiny pink doll. She was a little smaller than Annie at birth, but arrived with the same mop of brown curls and long brown eyelashes. (With time, I am hopeful of growing rather more reasonable about my Children's beauty, but you will agree with me, I am sure, Charlotte, that Mothers ought to be allowed to crow over their Infants without fear of the accusation of partiality!)

My Mother's letter on the arrival of Cassandra Jane more closely resembles a letter of condolence than one of congratulation. She hopes I am not too cast down at the birth of another girl and begs me to keep up my spirits. Her fervent wish is that I should not suffer her fate and be "burdened" with girls. Further, she prays that Mr. Darcy will not think less of his Wife for not producing an Heir. It is no use telling her that my Husband finds his Daughters a source of unending delight, that he is inordinately proud of them and plans to engage Mr. Thomas Lawrence to paint a family portrait as soon as convenient. It is profoundly irksome that one's own Mother does not share the blessing of the birth of a *healthy Child*. From Lady Catherine I expect little other than criticism—but let us leave it there, I shall not waste more good paper and ink on such a vexing matter.

Your own family news is wonderfully diverting and your description of Mr. Collins playing on the floor with young Robert at marbles is such that I might have been in the room myself. Are we not fortunate to have such happy, healthy Children?

Here, too, the weather has been bleak and miserable, but though there are few opportunities to be outdoors, we do not want for amusement. If nothing else, Miss Annie's attempts at dancing are most entertaining. She would not be half so funny if she did not take herself quite so seriously!

Dear Charlotte, in making light of my shortcomings as a correspondent, I would not wish you to think this a reflection of my regard for your friendship. You are so often in my thoughts and I treasure your letters almost as much as your affection. There are few people who own as much of my heart as you. I am resolved to mend my ways as I grow tired of having to apologise every time I put pen to paper.

As ever,

THE GREAT HOUSE
WEDNESDAY, 7th FEBRUARY, 1816

Dearest Husband,

Jane was brought to bed of a boy last evening, to be named George Edward. I believe he will be a fine Gentleman for he showed excellent manners in arriving in the early evening, and made a very short business of it. We are all grateful, with the sole exception of young Frederick Charles, who would prefer his Brother to be sent on his way with all haste! Now almost two, he seems to feel his position in the household to be in jeopardy. Poor little Frederick, he is finding life altogether unkind thus far! I suggested to Jane that perhaps his new Brother might bring a special present for Frederick's birthday next month, to make amends. Needless to say, Annie, so very fond of her elder Cousin, finds his behaviour most perplexing, but is very loyal, never crying when he takes toys from her, or won't play with her. Nurse assures me that this objectionable behaviour is perfectly normal in two- and three-year-olds, and will soon pass.

Your Daughter continues to be enamoured of her younger Sister—still her Rosebud. Nurse and I are mindful of not excluding her, and encourage Annie to help tend to Cassie. She is a happy Child; I have many a kiss in the course of the day, and many a laugh at her droll little ways. At bedtime she enquires after her Papa when she misses her goodnight kiss: When does Papa return? Will it be soon?

Lest you think I have joined the ranks of Lady Mansfield's regiment of women who talk of nothing but their Children, I shall cease forthwith! Nor should you think that my days are so occupied that I have no time to miss my dearest Love. Quite to the contrary, I assure you. Knowing that Jane is safe, I long to be home and for your own return some three days after—if the many pleasures of London do not contrive to delay you! Mr. Bingley begs me mention that he hopes to accept your invitation to shoot at Pemberley in March. George Edward's christening will probably take place the first week of the month and they will join us thereafter. The Daleys, too, if Margaret's Father is well enough to be left at home. Let us hope so.

While her concern for her Father is admirable, she is denied much pleasure as a consequence of her devotion to him. It would give me particular joy to have an opportunity of improving my acquaintance with that Family, but shall not indulge any expectation of it soon.

The weather here of late has been quite depressing: a little snow, much rain and howling winds. This morning, though it is really too muddy even for such a desperate walker as your Wife, I nevertheless braved the elements and took a short walk hereabouts, returning much refreshed having seen small signs of spring in the hedgerows. Are we not fortunate to have such beautiful countryside around us—how I pity you, my Dear, confined the whole day in dreary banks and offices, and a long list of commissions from an inconsiderate Wife. But no, I should not feel too sorrowful on your account when I recollect that the theatre, Almack's, Vauxhall, and all manner of diversions lie at your feet. Enjoy them all, my Love, but think fondly on the Woman who loves you above all others, who longs for your return and the warmth of your embrace—who else, but your

Pemberley
Friday, 19th April, 1816

My dear Aunt,

Thank you for your letter, which found me at the breakfast table with a sole companion, my dear Husband.

These past weeks we have enjoyed the considerable pleasure of having for company the Bingleys and Daleys. It was a very agreeable visit. There was everything to make it so: kindness, conversation and variety. Mr. Darcy had been keen to arrange a shooting party for the Gentlemen, so we fixed on March following Mr. Darcy's return from town and George Edward's christening. (Jane, you should know, has made a good recovery, though still a little pale.)

While the men were at their sport, we women found time to visit all the principal walks, including your favourite, the one around the top of the park. When the weather did not allow for sport, the men played at billiards.

Mrs. Daley, Margaret, was especially welcome. I have long wanted to know her better, but her loyalty to her Father is such that she is seldom from home as he is seldom in health. (I do not recall, have you met her at Pemberley? If you have heard all this before, pray excuse me.) Such devotion to a parent in a young, married woman might indicate a more staid manner than is the reality: she is very pleasant, cheerful and interested in everything about her, and at the same time showing a thoughtful, considerate and decided turn of mind. Fortunately, her devotion extends to her doting Husband, a Gentleman I have long admired, whose patience and forbearance with their domestic situation may even exceed her own.

We had lively discussions about the new novel, *Emma*, which by chance we had both lately read. Margaret did not like it so well as *Sense and Sensibility* and *Mansfield Park* by the same authoress. I, on the other hand, detested Fanny Price (as you well know) but the adorable Emma Woodhouse, despite (or perhaps because of) her many faults is so perfectly delightful, that I even forgive the authoress her dedication to the Prince Regent. I shall welcome your opinion when you next write. Mrs. Daley, by the bye, has heard rumours that the authoress is a Miss Austen, residing in Hampshire, and also tells me that Sir Walter Scott (upon whom we were able to agree!) has written a review of *Emma* in this month's *Quarterly Review*. Jane, who had not yet read *Emma*, disagreed vigorously with me on the simpering, virtuous Fanny Price, so you see we did not lack for spirited conversation or entertainment.

The Children, too, had great fun. One morning Annie and Frederick Charles were taken by their Fathers to the stables where they had such a time with the horses, squealing with excitement and laughter as they were hoisted upon their mounts and walked around the courtyard. Young Frederick appears to have accepted that his Brother is here to stay and is of a better disposition than when I last saw him. The two youngest Cousins eat and sleep and gurgle and cry and smile as well or better than other Infants, and are naturally a source of delight and wonder to their doting Mothers.

I trust this finds you and my Uncle and Cousins in good health.

Affectionately,
E.D.

Pemberley
Tuesday, 16th July, 1816

My dear Charlotte,

I was very glad of your letter this morning, for Annie keeping to her bed with a cold, which she generously gifted to her Father, has made us rather dull. Annie is most trying in her misery and refuses to understand why she may not see her Sister. Nurse and I attempt to entertain her with books, dolls and games, but none of these find favour for long. Otherwise, I am as well as one can expect to be in weather which deprives one of exercise; we have nothing but ceaseless rain and insufferable mud to complain of. Thankfully, the weather is my sole complaint for the hay was already brought in and the house has been fragrant with the scent of jams and jellies. The rain will swell the apples, no doubt, which may be of more importance to the world in general, but I selfishly long for a dry summer day to take myself on a long walk, with the reward of an incomparable view of the Peaks, of which I shall never tire, at the end of it.

Yes, I fear Mr. Collins's intelligence is correct, though I regret that the unfortunate circumstance has been made so public. I know not the extent of Mr. Collins' knowledge, but I have no secrets from you, dear Charlotte, and shall lay before you the whole, sorry story, leaving it to your discretion how much or how little of the following you feel obliged to share with others.

In a letter to Jane in April last, Lydia complained that she and Wickham, having had a miserable winter and spring (in part due to the cold weather but mostly due to pressing bills and debts) were in very low spirits and, needing to get away from the everyday tedium of the north, had in mind to set out for Bath, which they felt would restore them in every way. My Mother, having received a similar letter and agreeing wholeheartedly with the scheme, had hopes of improving upon it by persuading my Father to join them there. He, however, could not be prevailed upon, no matter how loudly and often she railed that his Wife's health and nerves were in pressing need of Bath's restorative waters. Chagrined, she sent Lydia a sum of money (without my Father's knowledge) to assist with their expenses, whereupon Lydia ordered new clothes, whose cost exceeded by several pounds the sum my Mother had sent, thereby adding to the burden of their debts.

She then applied to Jane for assistance, who despite her reservations about the wisdom of the whole venture, was forthcoming and sent money, cautioning, however, that it might be wiser to use these funds to clear their debts and pay their bills; and further suggesting (dear Jane!) that they might save the expense of travelling to Bath by coming to stay at The Great House. For her trouble and generosity Jane received neither acknowledgement nor thanks.

Nothing further was heard from them until the beginning of June when Jane received a letter from Lydia, postmarked in Bath, that Wickham, having at first won a great deal of money at the gambling tables, proceeded then to lose it, and more besides (for which, Lydia insisted, some disreputable officers were at fault—certainly not her Husband). Now they found themselves in such deeply compromising circumstances that the very real threat of debtors' prison lay before them!

Jane at once put the whole business before her Husband. The situation being beyond the scope of Mr.

Bingley's experience, they directly (and most unwillingly, having some limited knowledge of Mr. Darcy's past dealings with Mr. Wickham) applied to Mr. Darcy for advice. His immediate thought was to do nothing at all—a spell in debtors' prison at Bath might prove to be of more lasting benefit to the Wickhams than the waters, but upon reflection, and seeing our discomfort at the prospect of a Sister imprisoned, he undertook to engage the services of an attorney of his acquaintance in Bath, who might ascertain the extent and sum of these debts.

In due course, Mr. Tarnlow sent Mr. Darcy a long list (some three pages, closely written) of debtors with varying sums of money against their names. As he read, my Husband's face grew darker and darker with anger.

"Lizzy, were it not for you and your Sister Jane, I should not put forth one penny to satisfy these debts. They are a selfish, worthless couple, who do not deserve the effort and money it will take to sort out their costly muddles—and you know as well as I, Lizzy, they won't even thank us for our trouble, and will take it as their due! This will be the second time I have come to Wickham's aid and somehow I must make sure it is the last."

Kitty, meanwhile, informed us of the uproar at Longbourn. In desperation I suppose, Lydia had applied to my Mother for money, begging her to intercede with my

Father and send funds for their relief. Once again, Mamma's attempts to get him to rush off to Bath proved fruitless, and she took to her room. By now my Father was fully to blame for the disaster—had they been at Bath with the Wickhams, this could never have happened. First Brighton, now Bath, and her poor, poor Lydia, all alone and at the mercy of scurrilous ne'er-do-wells with no one to take her part, &c., &c. Moreover, by my Mother's reckoning, Mr. Darcy was also at fault, if you please—he should have immediately set out for Bath to settle the business. With his connections and money the whole matter would have been over in a trice! It appears that only Jane and Mr. Bingley were quite blameless.

The outcome of the sorry affair was that, through Mr. Tarnlow, Mr. Bingley and Mr. Darcy shared the expense of settling all outstanding bills and debts, saving Mr. Wickham not only from debtors' prison, but also from the embarrassment of losing his commission. There was, however, a proviso in the agreement which Mr. Wickham was required to sign: that henceforth his pay and any other income will be sent directly to Mr. Tarnlow, from which Mr. T. will settle their bills, pay their rent and send them a small spending allowance sufficient for their daily needs. Wickham has also undertaken not to borrow money. Should it be discovered that debts have been incurred of which Mr. Tarnlow was not apprised and which he feels are unwarranted, the Colonel of W.'s regiment will be immediately notified and may take whatever steps he feels necessary to safeguard the honour of the regiment. Wickham's Colonel has been made fully aware of these arrangements and of the circumstances which led to them. It is further stipulated that this is the last time either Mr. Darcy or Mr. Bingley will come to his aid.

Oh, Charlotte, how thankful I am that they yet have no Children, innocents who would surely suffer from the selfish acts of their Parents! When Lydia was here following Annie's birth, I distinctly recall her saying, "Thank goodness we have not yet been blessed with Children. We are having so much fun that we should have no time for them if we did."

We must now pray that in coming so close to the misery of a debtors' prison, they have seen the inevitable consequences of continuing to live their previous, foolish lives and will mend their ways. I wish I could believe it.

How time flies—your Robert William three; little Catherine Maria a year old already, Annie two last month, and Cassie seven months. Lest I forget: as promised, I have written Aunt Gardiner that you would be much obliged for the pattern of the jacket and trousers, or whatever it is, that boys wear when they are first put into breeches. I have asked that she send it to you directly. I suppose that since Lady C. had no boys, this is a subject upon which she has no valuable advice to share?

As ever, my dear Friend,
E.D.

PEMBERLEY
MONDAY, 16th SEPTEMBER, 1816

My dear Jane,

Pray, sit down. You will hardly believe what I am about to relate. Indeed, I can scarce believe it myself. Where to begin? Now, do not alarm yourself; there is no bad news. Not at all. No, no, it is good news, but of such a surprising nature that I am still recovering from the shock of it all. Such a to-do!

Forgive me, I am flustered and not in a proper state of mind. So, let me just state simply (for you would never guess)—our Sister, Mary, is engaged to be married! Her betrothed is a Mr. Dudley Digweed, a clerk in Uncle Philips' law office in Meryton, with "excellent prospects," she writes. (Mr. Digweed's prospects will surely improve even further and faster with this alliance to his employer's family? Of course, I do not mean to suggest that his reasons for marrying Mary are purely practical in nature, so do not trouble yourself to scold me.)

Regrettably, Mary writes little more about Mr. Digweed than I have already related—no mention of his age, height, looks, character, income—merely adding that he shares her interest in music, and understands and respects the importance of her studies, which he insists she must continue after they are wed. I dare say we must be patient and hope that Kitty will furnish the particulars. However, I think we may safely assume that the Gentleman, as well as musical and studious in character, is also *impetuous* and *thrifty*, for Mary writes that a short engagement is planned (the banns are to be read next month). A wedding journey following the ceremony is not foreseen, and the wedding itself will be as simple as possible. Further, excessive frivolous expenditure is to be avoided at all costs. (This last direction must have pleased our Father immensely, do you not think?) A postscript adds that she expects neither of us to attend the marriage ceremony, but *should* we feel inclined to mark the occasion, a monetary gift would be most suitable.

By the bye, Mary asked me to relate these tidings to you (though our Mother, she added, admonished her severely for her ill-manners in doing so—rightly insisting that the occasion demanded individual announcements, especially to one's own Sisters. Further, if she insisted upon only one announcement for the two of us, it should properly be addressed to you as the Eldest). Upon consideration, however, Mary decided that since she now has even less time to spare than previously, and since your two *Boys* must be more tiresome and demanding than my two *Girls*, I would naturally have more time at my disposal to write!

Well, now that I have now done my Sisterly duty, I suppose I can retire to my sofa for the rest of the day.

Ever yours,
E.D.

Pemberley
Thursday, 19th September, 1816

Dearest Jane,

I hasten to acquaint you with the contents of a letter from Kitty, received just this morning. As I feared, poor Kitty is mortified that Mary should be marrying before she herself does, and writes that Mary, in her newly affianced state, behaves insufferably, wasting no opportunity to remind Kitty of her superior position in the Family now that she is betrothed. Not that Kitty is jealous of Mr. Digweed; indeed, she is at pains to make that quite clear. She describes him as an ambitious man of about thirty, with thinning hair, a slight stoop and bad breath. Further, he is ingratiating and over-eager to please, yet at the same time inordinately pleased with himself. (Does this description not remind you of our—or perhaps I should say my—first impressions of our Cousin, Mr. Collins? Sadly, though, Mr. Digweed has no expectations of the kind Mr. Collins looks forward to in inheriting Longbourn.)

Kitty, it would seem, was his first choice, but having made the Gentleman aware that his attentions were received neither with any pleasure, nor reciprocated, he wasted no time in turning his attentions to Mary where his compliments were more enthusiastically received.

My Mother has been of little consolation, letting it be known that Kitty, not Mary, will now be the companion of her later years. Indeed, it is quite the joke in the neighbourhood and our Sister is quite beside herself with mortification. Poor Kitty! I have just now written some lines of consolation and shall also request of our Mother that Kitty be permitted to come to Pemberley on 1st December, and shall contrive that her presence is desired until my lying-in in February. Surely Mamma cannot refuse? I know you will agree that we must protect Kitty from our Mother's selfishness, and Mary's superiority, and her own perceived humiliation.

My greatest fear is that in desperation Kitty may make an unsuitable marriage in order to escape from Longbourn. Let you and I have her here, near us, where we may direct her towards the patience and wisdom of waiting for a suitable match where mutual affection supercedes all other attractions. Were Mr. Darcy a penniless curate, I would love him not one whit less. I feel certain, too, that were he a tinker, you would love and respect Mr. Bingley every bit as much as you do today. I pray that our Sister, Kitty, will know our joy and not be denied the rewards of a partnership based on mutual trust, love, respect and companionship.

Ever yours,

E.D.

PEMBERLEY

THURSDAY, 19th SEPTEMBER, 1816

Dearest Sister,

I beg you not to distress yourself. This is one of those occasions inflicted upon us as a reminder that life is not intended to be a state of perfect happiness, and there is little I can write in consolation that your own fortitude will not more readily suggest.

There is no reason to think, dearest Kitty, that because Mary will be shortly married, you will be obliged to remain at Longbourn with our Mother. Having said thus much, I agree that, hitherto, it appeared that Mary might have remained unmarried and at Longbourn, but it was by no means certain that this would be the case. Pray, do not rush to seek a partner for life. You are an attractive young woman of fine mind and character, and I entreat you not to be hasty in choosing a Husband. Yes, I say *choosing* a husband! Do not compromise yourself by making do with the next man to ask for your hand. You have no need to be grateful to somebody for singling you out; indeed the Gentleman of right mind and sensibility who is worthy of you will be full of gratitude in the knowledge that *you* have done him the very great honour by accepting *him!*

Be in no doubt of the seriousness of my words, dear Sister. My fondest hope is that you will find the happiness in marriage that Jane and I have found; I wish nothing less for you than a partner in life with whom you may share mutual love and respect. Real happiness depends upon it, and I entreat you to accept nothing less. The world may consider a good match merely a practical matter of pounds per annum income, but I pray you will be wiser.

I shall write to our Mother and request that you be allowed to come here as soon as is possible following Mary's nuptials, shall we say beginning 1st December? This will allow our Mother a full month of your company after Mary's departure. Little Cassie celebrates her first birthday on 16th December and it is only fitting that her Godmother should be on hand. It would be hardly proper to send you back to Longbourn before the Christmas festivities, then I feel certain that Jane would wish you to be at The Great House for George's first birthday on 6th February. After all, your Godmotherly duties extend to him also. Indeed, I do not think Jane and I could bear to part with you before the first of April, a full four months' absence from Longbourn, during which time our Mother will have become quite used to shifting for herself for entertainment and companionship.

Take heart, my dear Sister, and do not fret that you are the last of the five Bennet girls to be wed. Rather, rejoice that your Sisters are happy, and look forward to the day, whenever that may be (but rest assured that it *will* be) when your own happiness equals theirs.

Affectionately,

PEMBERLEY

FRIDAY, 22[d] NOVEMBER, 1816

Dearest Kitty,

Thank you for the unexpected pleasure of your letter yesterday. As I like unexpected pleasures, it made me very happy. A note arrived from the Norland girls in the same post as yours, asking when you arrive.

Expect a most agreeable letter from me—for not being overburdened with subject (having nothing at all to say) I shall have no check to my genius!

Your account of Mary's wedding is most strange, though upon reflection, given Mary's distaste for displays of affection, perhaps it is not quite so odd after all. Nevertheless, one might have expected even Mary to allow herself to step out of character on her wedding day!

From what you say, my Father was the most joyful of the wedding party.

Dear Kitty, calm yourself about Mr. Digweed, now your Brother—merely be as civil to him as his bad breath permits and politeness dictates. As for Mary, I fear she will have to take up a new subject for study if she is to run an efficient household. That a maid has already jilted her and hired herself elsewhere is worrisome. Until now, Mary has never had to concern herself with household matters, holding herself aloof from such earthly concerns in her pursuit of higher learning. Moreover, her complaint that as a newly-married woman she is *burdened* with the infinity of compliments and civilities she must pay and receive is yet another indication of the urgent need for her to study politeness and respect for others as carefully as she would examine one of Mr. Fordyce's sermons.

The weather has been cold but fine and we hope it will continue dry until you are safely here. We look forward to your arrival here with great anticipation. Your Goddaughter looks forward to making her Aunt Kitty's acquaintance and asks several times daily if it is tomorrow that she comes.

I can recollect nothing more to say at present; perhaps breakfast may assist my ideas.

I was deceived—my breakfast supplied only two ideas:

One is to request some flower seeds from Longbourn. It would give me so much pleasure to see familiar favourites from home in my own beds next summer. Pray tell Mr. Hill that I would particularly like to have mignionette seed if they can be spared.

Secondly, last time you came you packed with more haste than judgement, so let me remind you not to be so intent upon merely *filling* the trunk!

I shall now leave you and write to the Norland girls to invite them to join us. I also have no doubt that their Uncle will welcome the excuse of your visit for another of the parties he is so fond of arranging.

Ever yours,

1817

PEMBERLEY

FRIDAY, 7TH FEBRUARY, 1817

My dear Kitty,

I have received your letter, and suppose you expect me to be displeased with its contents? At first, I confess I was much disappointed by your proposed lengthened stay at The Great House since I had felt sure that February would not pass quite away without bringing you back to Pemberley. Observing my preoccupation at breakfast, and enquiring of the reason, Mr. Darcy proposed a visit to The Great House ourselves! He is anxious to shoot with Mr. Bingley, we could all celebrate Frederick Charles's third birthday together, Annie and Cassie could play with their Cousins, and we three Sisters could amuse ourselves at leisure—a simple, wonderful scheme to please us all. We have in mind to come on the 22nd at about four o'clock and will leave after Frederick's birthday, for as you know, we are to leave for town at the end of the month, returning you to Longbourn en route.

Your letter mentions a curate several times, but in such vague terms that my curiosity was at once aroused. And might this Gentleman be the foremost reason for wishing to delay your return to Pemberley? Or must I find out for myself when I come?

That you have been working a footstool for me is a most agreeable surprise and I shall value it so much as a proof of your affection and industry that I may never have the heart to put my feet upon it! Therefore, I shall work a muslin case in satin stitch to keep it from the dirt and thus can proudly display before company your loving work in its pristine state. Thank you, dear Kitty.

As ever,

Lizzy

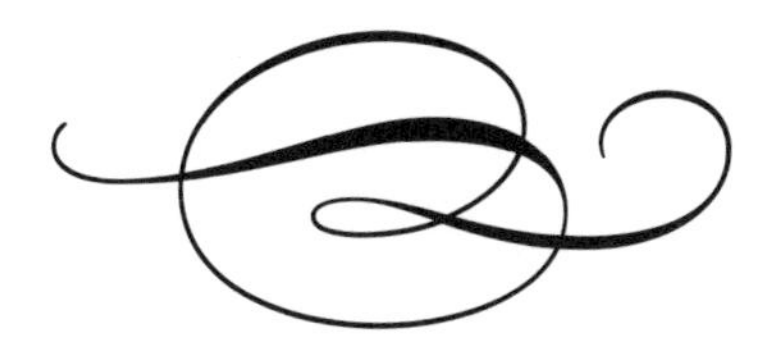

PEMBERLEY

SATURDAY, 22[d] FEBRUARY, 1817

My dear Jane,

With this letter I must commend my Husband and Daughter to your care. I regret that I must remain at Pemberley. Cassie is just now recovering from a severe attack of the croup and is not yet well enough to travel even the relatively short distance to The Great House. Since we are to journey to town just several weeks hence, Mr. Brownley advises that she rest quietly here to avoid the possibility of a chill and to ensure that she regains her full health before our departure to London. (By the bye, it may be worthwhile to inform you that Mr. Brownley ordered taking two grains of calomel every hour until the symptoms subside, and then gradually lessening the dose.)

I shall think of you all. You will never be far from my thoughts.

E.D.

Grosvenor Street, London
Sunday, 27th April, 1817

Dearest Jane,

I thank you for your long letter, which I will endeavour to deserve by relating the particulars of last evening's party. As you know, I am no lover of London society and parties (and secretly often still feel out of place) but I must say that ours went off extremely well. Above 80 people were invited, including, of course, my dear Uncle and Aunt Gardiner, and Georgiana and her Husband. There were the usual vexations beforehand, of course, but at last everything was quite right. The rooms were dressed up with flowers &c., and looked very pretty.

The musicians arrived at half past seven and by eight the company began to appear. Including everybody we were almost 100, which was more than we had expected, and quite enough to fill the back drawing room and leave a few to be scattered about in the other. The music was extremely good, and all the performers gave great satisfaction. The house was not clear until after 12, after which we retired immediately to bed. You will also wish to know that I wore the new white gown, made very much like my yellow one, which you always told me sat very well—also the pretty diamond Darcy tiara. My Aunt looked most stylish in dove grey silk overlaid with lace of the same shade, and hair dressed with three ostrich feathers of differing lengths, artfully arranged. Georgiana was simply though fashionably attired in a plain, cream silk, the neckline edged in seed pearls—I dare say we were the three most elegant ladies present!

Georgiana and the Colonel have been here at Grosvenor Street during most of our stay, making London immensely more tolerable than usual. They are both such good company and perfect guests with their quiet ways and manners. While Georgiana looks as well as ever, I did at times notice an almost imperceptible veil of melancholy about her, so contrived that we should spend some private time together that I might either pry out the cause, or satisfy myself that my imaginings hold no cause for alarm. Colonel Fitzwilliam had similarly hinted to me his concern that something was amiss. A morning came when the Gentlemen were from home and the weather confined us indoors. Her protestations that all was perfectly well were so violent that I was convinced I was right, and persisted in my enquiries. At last, she confessed her fear that she is unable to give the Colonel Children. We set aside our blushes and spoke frankly upon the subject. It was my opinion that while they have been married almost two years, that in itself does not prove her fear. She had shrunk from speaking to her Husband, and from consulting the Fitzwilliam physician, hoping that an opportunity might arise for them come to Pemberley, where she could consult Brownley, whom she knows and trusts. Agreeing that, unpleasant as the notion may be, a medical consultation was the only means of putting her fears to rest, we decided to ask the Darcys' London physician (whom G. has also known since childhood, though not as well as Mr. Brownley) to wait upon us here in Grosvenor Street and seek his advice. We further settled it that, for the time being at least, the appointment would be our secret alone.

Mr. Clark arrived on the due date, and after a thorough examination declared that he saw no reason in the world why Georgiana should not bear as many Children as she desired! You should have seen us, Jane, holding hands and dancing around the room, by turns laughing and crying. Nurse and Annie happened to pass the open door at that very moment, so we each took one of Annie's hands and swung her around the room. Bewildered at first, then, seeing us laughing so much, she caught our spirit, laughing as her little legs tried to keep up with us. We were still dancing when the Gentlemen returned, much to their astonishment, but we refused to state the reason for our gaiety, no matter how hard they tried to winkle it from us!

I have since extracted a promise from G. that she will never keep such a problem to herself again. If, for reasons of delicacy, she cannot discuss something with her Husband, she must write to me and we will unravel it together.

What dreadful, unseasonal hot weather we have! It keeps one in a continual state of inelegance. I hope it will be a tolerable afternoon for I have promised to take Annie for a drive in Hyde Park (she would dearly love to see the Prince out riding!) and if the weather continues so hot she will not be in the best of tempers, I fear. She has lately become most perverse and saucy, her favourite words being shan't, can't, won't, etc. Nurse assures me this is natural behaviour which she will soon outgrow—how very much I want to believe it! It cannot be too soon.

About your commissions: For the summer gowns I have purchased plain brown cambric muslin for morning wear; the other, a very pretty periwinkle and white cloud (mine is yellow and white), seven yards for you and seven-and-one-half yards for me (being taller).

We leave in two days. It is much too late to be in London, especially knowing that the countryside is at its finest this time of year, but it couldn't be helped. It is far preferable to remaining alone at P., but nevertheless, I long to be home again.

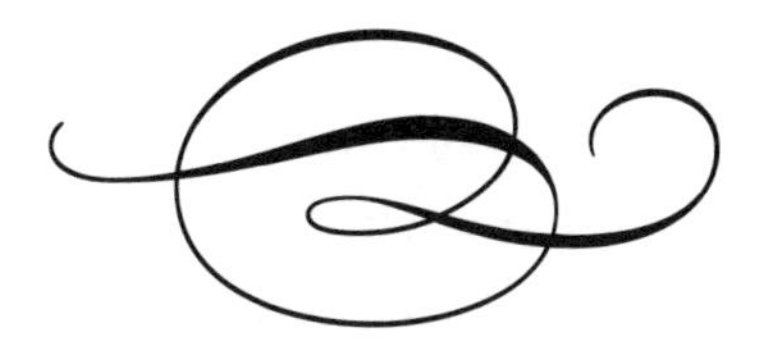

Pemberley
Tuesday, 10th June, 1817

My dear Aunt,

Where shall I begin? Which of all my unimportant nothings shall I tell you first? As I write, my dear Husband fishes for trout. Annie and I have just returned from a walk to find him—she has inherited her Mother's love of walking, and at the great age of three years and three days, tries very hard to keep up even when her short legs show every sign of collapse (I fear she may also have inherited her Mother's stubbornness). It would have amused you to see our progress; in climbing a hill, Miss Annie only with difficulty keeps pace with me, yet would not flinch for the world. On level ground she is almost my equal; on the slope down to the stream she scampers ahead. We always stop to look at flowers and listen to birds and watch passing clouds—I think it right to take pains to cultivate the eyes and ears of Children for nature. Moreover, nothing tends more to health than exercise and air, and the more Children are out of the house the better. (If there is any subject on which I feel diffident, it is that my affection for my Children will lead me to take too much care of them. Mr. Darcy has been instructed to tell me if I show any tendency towards the kind of suffocating Mothering practised by Lady Mansfield!)

Cassie, at eighteen months, shows every sign of becoming a natural, open hearted, affectionate little girl, adored by her elder Sister. I fervently hope that they will become loving friends as they grow up together. To be able to call a Sister one's best Friend is truly a blessing, a gift I cherish dearly and one I would wish my Daughters to know.

Haymaking is now over and if the weather continues fair, Barford expects the corn to ripen early this year. Mr. Darcy cautions against hiring extra workers for another six weeks at least; Barford fears that if it is left too late, there will be no extra workers available to help with the harvest. Such, you see, are the burning issues at Pemberley—I cannot imagine dilemmas of this nature arising in Gracechurch Street!

How envious I am that you are to visit Longbourn—and how sorry that time will not permit you to come further north to Derbyshire! I should so dearly love to see you and my dear Uncle. But I do not despair entirely, for we are to visit Jane at the end of this month and remain there until her lying-in. In my mind's eye I already see the Cousins playing together, our Husbands spending leisurely days fishing, and Jane and I enjoying lazy, unhurried days of reading, conversation, sewing, and whatever our fancies lead us to. Only your presence could improve upon our scheme, my dear Aunt!

Yours ever,

E.D.

PEMBERLEY

SATURDAY, 28th JUNE, 1817

My dear Jane,

To make long sentences upon unpleasant subjects is very odious, and I shall therefore get rid of the one now uppermost in my thoughts as soon as possible—we must delay our departure. There, it is said, much as it disappoints me to have to record it at all.

Yesterday morning at four o'clock I was awoken by Nurse, alarmed by my darling Cassie screaming in pain. Rushing to the nursery, I found her just as Nurse had described, quite purple in the face with pain and her little body hot with fever. Mr. Darcy ordered Brownley to be sent for immediately. By the time he got here, Cassie had calmed somewhat and the fever appeared to be abating, but she appeared to be still in pain, for which Brownley could find no apparent cause. Finally, spent and exhausted, she fell asleep. Brownley said the longer she rests the better, she may well sleep off her disorder.

I stayed by her bedside throughout the day and by last evening she seemed much improved, even managing to smile at me, twice! I was heartened enough to leave her in the care of Nurse through the night, though with instructions to wake me should there be any change. This morning, Mr. Brownley advises not leaving home until Cassie's strength returns, a day or two, he says. Otherwise he is satisfied with her improvement.

I have been urging Mr. Darcy to depart with Annie, for I know he has looked forward to our visit as much as I have, but he insists that we will make the journey together. So, expect us all on 2nd July, towards two o'clock!

Affectionately,

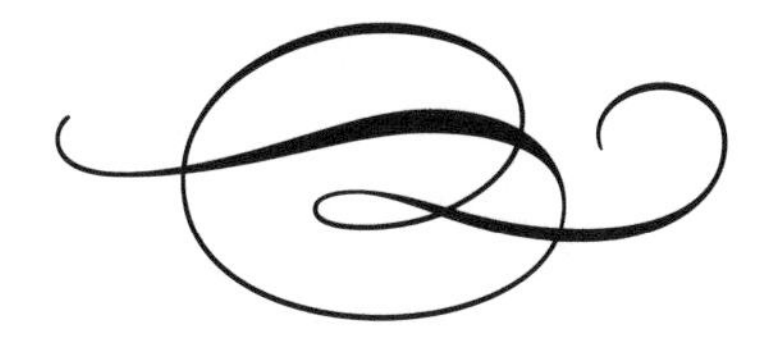

PEMBERLEY

TUESDAY, 1st JULY, 1817

My dear Jane,

I regret we are obliged to postpone our visit once again. My darling Cassie was taken ill again early yesterday morning with a fever. It is a grievous blow to our spirits for she had been making such good progress. I was at her side all day and by evening she had rallied again and slept the night through. This morning, she is weak from exhaustion, to be sure, but assured by Mr. Brownley that she is out of danger.

We are all quite fatigued and long for the restorative powers which your good company will surely bestow. I shall send an express when we are finally able to leave Pemberley.

With love,

Lizzy

PEMBERLEY
THURSDAY, 10th JULY, 1817

My dear Jane,

I know you will forgive this short letter and the prior absence of news from me when I tell you that since Cassie fell ill, I have not left her side for more than an hour altogether. Her condition has given us all serious cause for alarm: when she is awake, the fever gives her so much discomfort and distress; when she sleeps too long, I begin to fear she will never awaken—a feeling impossible to describe. I hold her hot little body to my breast to soothe her, but she cannot settle for long. Brownley maintains that the fever will break soon, that we must be patient. How easy to say, how difficult to accomplish!

(My Husband insists that I join him for breakfast now. While I have little appetite to bring to the table, I must not add to his worries and shall attempt to eat a little to satisfy him.)

11th July, 1817

Good news, Jane! The fever has abated once more and my darling Girl rests comfortably. Brownley declares she is now quite safe. How pitiful she looks, so pale and thin, but with fresh air and nourishment, in a few months she will be well again. It is such a relief to cast this weight from our shoulders. At times during these past days and weeks, I thought—but no matter, it is over and we are all ready to be happy again.

My poor Annie has been sorely neglected—despite my efforts to spend time with her each day, I have been so fatigued and distracted with worry that she has gained little satisfaction from my presence. Today, however, we have played at spillikins, paper ships, riddles and cards, and later I have promised her we shall gather flowers and make a posy for Cassie.

With love,

E.

PEMBERLEY
FRIDAY, 18th JULY, 1817

My dear Jane,

How can I bear to write these terrible words? In writing them, perhaps they will seem real at last, perhaps I will feel their full, awful import. Perhaps I will feel something, anything but this cold numbness which covers me like a shroud. This morning, just after dawn, Cassandra Jane, our dearest Cassie, aged one year and seven months, passed away peacefully, finally released from the ravages of the fever which consumed her tiny body.

Last evening, she was suddenly taken worse. Mr. Brownley was sent for and said she could not outlive the night. To see her little wasted body lying in a state of exhaustion cut to my very soul. This was once my lovely

Cassie. Against Mr. Brownley's and Mr. Darcy's wishes and advice, I insisted upon holding her in my arms, and there at last she expired, peacefully, with her face on my breast. I gave her one last kiss and she was taken from me. My sweet, darling Girl. Gone. My head rings with Why? Why? Why? I get no answer. And still I ask, Why? Why? Why was my darling taken from me? She did no wrong, she scarce ever cried, not even as the fever raged, nor when she cut her first teeth, even when she tumbled and cut her head taking her first steps. Why is this world so cruel?

Forgive me, dearest Jane, for inflicting my despair on you. I know you will understand how much it means to be able to express it to you. I must not add to Mr. Darcy's own grief, yet I am so frightened of tomorrow and of all the tomorrows we must face without that dear person, who will be forever one year and seven months, who will be forever absent from our lives, never to experience the thrill of the wind in her hair running through the woods on a fine spring morning, the excitement of her first ball, the pride in writing her name for the very first time.

How can I comfort my Husband on the loss of an adored Daughter? How can I comfort Annie, distraught at the loss of a Sister and frightened of dying herself? How can I comfort myself? Even though I would prefer to withdraw from life—yes, from even my adored Family—to the silence of my own room, I cannot. I owe it to them to guide us all from this day into the one that follows, and the one that follows after.

I *must* put down my pen and go to the nursery.

I *must* gather my living Child into my arms.

I *must* go to the library where I know I will find my Husband seeking solace among his books.

We *must* help each other somehow.

We *must* get through the dark days and nights ahead.

We *must* continue living; it cannot be otherwise.

Dear Jane, how I wish you were here, but I forbid you to contemplate it so close to your due time. Be assured that I will write to you often. Share our sorrow, but do not worry about us.

E.D.

PEMBERLEY

SUNDAY, 20th JULY, 1817

Thank you, dear Jane, for the comfort of your letter. There are very few people able to supply real comfort, but your heartfelt words succeeded. I, too, long for the warmth of your Sisterly embrace, but it cannot be, and the pen must suffice. I am relieved to know that you are in good health.

You ask about Mr. Darcy. What can I say? I know not how to comfort him. Indeed our shared sorrow has made us strangers and we can give each other no solace. Is that not strange? We have each withdrawn into that private part of our souls to which we alone possess the keys, to which no other may gain entry; that place where grief reigns mistress and demands our all. Yet the loss of our Child is no less agonizing for the absence of hysterical expression. I am grateful that my pen continues to write even as my tongue fails me, and more than grateful that I may pen my despair openly to you. Would that this same pen could find words adequate to tell you how very, very thankful I am for such a loving, understanding Sister.

As I go about the house, I see her everywhere, Jane; it sinks my very heart to enter the nursery. Yet where can I go at Pemberley that I shall not be reminded of my darling Girl? As so often, I turn to George Crabbe to take stock:

Why do I live, when I desire to be
At once from life and life's long labour free?
Like leaves in spring, the young are blown away
Without the sorrows of a slow decay,
I, like you withered leaf, remain behind
Nipp'd by the frost, and shivering in the wind.

Death casts such a long shadow; it seems to touch everyone at Pemberley, yet our lives have not stopped. There are mourning clothes to be arranged for ourselves and for the servants. Mrs. Reynolds has already given directions for cloth to be dyed and crape to be purchased. The funeral takes place the day after tomorrow.

Mr. Kirkland mentioned Cassie by name at church this morning and has called several times. I am sure he means well, he is a kind man, yet I long to cry out that he cannot possibly understand my loss: he has been spared the grief of losing a Child; he cannot know a Mother's love and attachment to the Child she has borne; and the words he quotes from the Bible, intended to give me comfort, fall upon cold, barren soil. I wish him gone as soon as he is arrived. It is unkind of me, I know, and I trust my uncharitable nature is not too obvious to him.

The present would be unendurable without my Family to keep my eyes fixed firmly on the future, but, oh, Jane, how hard it is to envision that future without her.

Keep us in your prayers,
Elizabeth

Pemberley

Tuesday, 22d July, 1817

My dear Jane,

It is done. We laid our Darling to rest this morning. You will forgive me that I feel unable to write more—there is nothing I can write about this day that you cannot as well imagine yourself.

I am tired of letter-writing; perhaps a little repose may restore my regard for a pen. Pray, do not fret. I am well, but exhausted.

As ever,

E.D.

PEMBERLEY
SUNDAY, 27th JULY, 1817

My dear Jane,

When I received word of the express from Mr. Bingley this morning, you will hardly wonder that I was beside myself with anxiety, knowing that your lying-in was not for some weeks yet. Mr. Darcy assured me (as soon as I allowed him—which was several minutes later, and then only after I had ventured several imagined disasters which must have befallen you or your Family, each of which he was required to deny before I ventured another) that all was well and that you had been brought to bed of a fine Girl.

I congratulate you, dear Jane, on a Sister for Frederick and George, and beg you will believe me when I say that my joy on your safe delivery and the birth of a welcome Niece is not diminished, even though the event follows so shortly after my greatest sorrow. That my Niece shares my own name and that of the Cousin she will never have the pleasure of knowing gives me very great comfort and enormous pride, I assure you, and I thank you for the fine compliment.

Annie is at my side and begs me to add that she longs to see Elizabeth Cassandra and wishes Frederick and George to know that Mrs. Reynolds' Mittens had five kittens on Thursday last, and that her Papa has said she may have one for her very own, to be called Parsley. To own the truth, her Papa and I are indebted to Mittens for this timely diversion from the gloom which overshadows Pemberley. Mrs. Reynolds, bless her, encourages Annie to visit the kittens as often as possible and Annie regales us with reports of their antics. Three years old is too young to dwell upon death for too long, and while we attempt to be our normal selves in her presence, I doubt that Annie is deceived.

Yours,

E. Darcy

Pemberley

Wednesday, 30th July, 1817

Dearest Sister,

We visited her grave this morning, Mr. Darcy and I. The excursion was neither planned nor spoken of previously, yet when my Husband offered to accompany me on a walk, our steps led us to the cemetery of their own will. The day's warm sunshine seemed to mock us as we stood there quietly together staring at the wilting flowers atop that pile of earth beneath which lies our Daughter. We lingered just a few moments. Not a word was said; the press of our hands together more than sufficed.

Returning to the house, Nurse informed us that Annie was distraught, insisting on a funeral for her favourite doll, Rosebud, who had just died. With our permission, she suggested, might not a "funeral" help Annie with her own grief at the loss of an adored Sister. After consoling Annie, Mr. Darcy and I agreed and this afternoon, with a great deal of formality and garlands of flowers kindly gathered by Hopwith, in a box provided by Mrs. Reynolds, Annie laid her beloved Rosebud to rest in a grave dug by Johnson, an under-gardener, in a spot carefully chosen by Annie herself which she can see from the nursery. It was a short, very affecting ceremony conducted by Annie herself: the first lines of the Lord's Prayer, which she is presently learning, followed by an approximation of the first verse of Nurse's favourite hymn, which she hears daily in the nursery. The chief mourners were the two of us, Mrs. Reynolds, Nurse, Hopwith and several maids who were not immediately required elsewhere.

Afterwards, I accompanied Nurse and Annie to the nursery where Annie almost immediately fell into a deep sleep. Thus reassured, I withdrew to my bedchamber. Only moments later, that thick ice wall which has surrounded my heart finally shattered, releasing torrents of grief and the tears I had hitherto been unable to shed. I thought I was weeping quietly and unheard, but the next thing I recall is my Beloved taking me into his arms and holding me closely until the tears were spent.

Next, I find I am lying on my bed, and observe Mr. Darcy in conversation with Mr. Brownley, who is holding a small bottle and appearing to console my Husband. I recall wondering, What could they possibly have to discuss in my bedchamber? The bottle must have contained a strong sleeping draft, for when I next awoke it was morning and I saw Mrs. Reynolds herself drawing the curtains.

"Where is Flora? Is she unwell?" I asked, puzzled at my maid's absence.

"She is in perfect health, Ma'am," replied Mrs. R. "I was concerned, indeed the entire household was concerned to know—that is to say—I—we, were worried—after yesterday—that I thought it best …"

We were both spared prolonged embarrassment by my darling Annie bounding into the room and jumping on my bed, followed by Nurse.

"Excuse me, Mrs. Darcy, I told Miss Annie, Mamma was not to be disturbed, but she scampered away when I had my back turned …"

Reassuring Nurse that no harm was done, I took my naughty Annie into my arms, thanked Mrs. Reynolds for her concern and begged her to assure the household of my good health and my profound gratitude for their kindness and consideration during the past difficult days.

And so, dear Jane, let me reassure you, too, that I am at peace. I am determined not to dwell upon the past with melancholy and tears, but to think of my sweet Cassie with smiles, remembering the joy she brought us for such a short time. To avoid thinking of the past, I shall immerse myself in the present, mindful of the abundance of gifts with which I have been blessed. She will never be far from my thoughts, but I have in mind to write to Mr. Repton about planting a laburnum walk in her memory. Those pendulous blossoms dancing on a summer day will remind others of the happiness she gave us all.

Tomorrow, I shall pay a visit to Mrs. Barford, who has been much on my mind of late, and to whom I must make amends for my callous words upon the death of her Infant Son. I blush to recall what I said as I urged her to set her grief aside—that she was at least fortunate in not having to bear the burden of *years* of happy memories of her Child; that she had three other healthy Children. How those words haunt me now! Were I to have *ten* more, my grief at losing Cassie will not be lessened, ever. There will always be a special place in my heart that is hers alone.

Pray tell Mr. Bingley that Mr. Darcy's refusal of his invitations is no reflection upon Mr. Darcy's regard for him, I assure you. My Husband is withdrawn into himself and not even I seem able to offer any comfort. He is so accustomed to being in command of every situation, great and small, that it falls hard when life takes the reins from him.

Let me now hasten to the library in the hope of finding Mr. Darcy. Perhaps, at last, we can put into words what we have been unable to say to each other, words of consolation, and words of hope that brighter days will dawn. In saying them and repeating them often, we may actually come to believe them.

As always,
E.D.

PEMBERLEY
WEDNESDAY, 8th OCTOBER, 1817

My dear Charlotte,

I will endeavour to make this letter more worthy your acceptance than my last, though my abilities decrease and I have no more notion of penning a smart letter than of making a smart cap. I endeavour, as I must, to submit graciously to the will of providence and begin each new day with good intentions, yet by breakfast time usually find my anger rising and my spirits lowered. My poor, dear Family little know of what passes in my mind, and I am truly glad of it. Mr. Darcy at last makes a tolerable recovery, having given me grave cause for concern with his long, dreadful, deafening silences. I had feared I would never reach him again, but he is returned to me, thank goodness. Yes, we are both bruised and damaged, but more than ever united.

Annie is enchanted with her kitten, Parsley, and by day appears to be her normal little self once more, yet she has grown afraid of the dark. We agreed (Nurse and I—she is a remarkable woman of good sense and I have been so grateful for her reassuring presence, for my own as well as Annie's sake) to deal most tenderly with her. All of us (her Father, too) have taken to walking about the house with her without a candle, and talking and telling stories and enjoying the quiet dark. Parsley, previously dispatched to Mrs. Reynolds' room at bedtime, is now allowed to stay in the nursery at night. When I look in before retiring, it is such a precious picture to behold, these two small creatures curled up side by side contentedly.

My Mother and Father and Kitty spent a full six weeks in the neighbourhood, mostly at The Great House, where they had been expected for Elizabeth Cassandra's christening, and where, I dare say, Kitty had expectations of renewing her acquaintance with one Mr. Perrot, a curate whom she met on her earlier visit this year. I have not yet had the pleasure of meeting him.

My Mother had in mind to remain at Pemberley for several weeks, but my Father sensibly persuaded her that a visit of several days only would be far more appropriate at this time. How grateful I was for my dear, wise Father! I could not have borne it, I know. My Mother's notion of comfort would have offered me no solace at all, quite the reverse. It was finally agreed that they would arrive in time for the opening of partridge season, which would be a very welcome diversion for Mr. Darcy also, who might otherwise not have bothered at all. Thus, my Father and Mr. Darcy were happily occupied in the fields and not inconvenienced by the melancholy company of we women. All in all, it was a tolerable visit of just five days.

Yet, how strange it was, Charlotte—I had been in expectation of my Mother smothering me with condolences and platitudes and empty words of comfort. The reality, however, was that it was I who was expected to comfort *her*! She spent a good part of every day in tears bemoaning the loss of a beloved Grand-daughter and taking most meals in her room. Her nerves would not allow her to visit the grave, nor even to enter the nursery where she feared she would be overcome with grief. Poor Annie, how she longed to show her kitten to her Grandmamma, but not even a little girl's entreaties would persuade her! (Another source of profound grief for my Mother was that Mrs. Hill had had the wrong gown dyed black, but I shall not bore you with the particulars of that lengthy, daily subject.)

In a perverse manner, however, my Mother's behaviour did me a power of good. Rather than make me angry, the absurdity of her misplaced grief served to calm me. Mr. Darcy, too, benefited as much from my Father's companionship, as from the exercise and fresh air, and was in far better spirits afterwards. Together, the three of us visited Cassie's grave one morning. My Father was clearly much affected, demonstrating more real sorrow than my Mother's rivers of tears ever could.

Dear Charlotte, how pleased I am that your growing Family stays healthy and happy. Even more, your letters have an air of contentment with life that gives me very great pleasure.

Pray, tell Mr. Collins how very much obliged I am for his prayers on my Family's behalf. I must confess (*between ourselves only, Charlotte!*) that since Cassie was taken from me my relationship with God has suffered exceedingly; my anger and hurt render me quite incapable of forgiveness. I am therefore particularly grateful to Mr. Collins for his intercession on my behalf.

As ever,

E. Darcy

1818

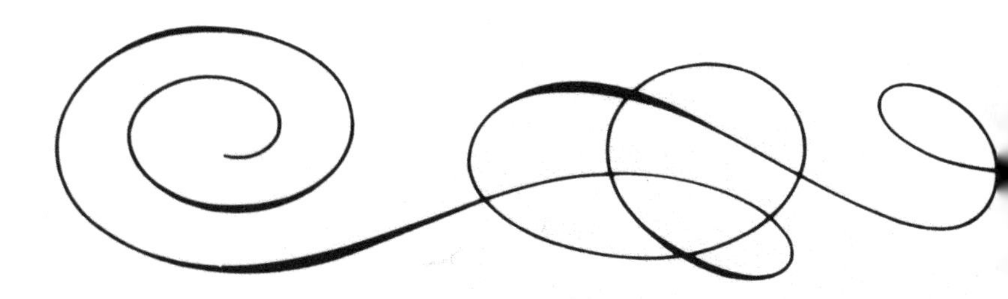

Pemberley
Thursday, 8th January, 1818

Dearest Jane,

How thankful I was to bid farewell to 1817! How glad I am that the Christmas season is over at last! Enduring the festive season of good will when one feels good will towards nobody is an exhausting business. For Annie's sake we wore brave faces, of course. On Christmas Eve, as a special treat, I took her with me to deliver poor baskets. She considered the morning a great adventure; for myself, it would have been better to have had the servants do it—the recipients of our largesse were so awkward in their thanks, not knowing what to say, whether to mention our loss or to ask how we fared. By the end of it all, I felt I should almost apologise for appearing at their doors, though I must own that

Annie herself proved a happy diversion, especially if the families had Children of her own age. She is certainly not shy! Now Jane, be assured I do not sit here soaking in a warm tub of self-pity. I cannot think why I even mentioned the business with the poor baskets, but really cannot persuade myself to start this letter afresh.

Believe me, we are all making good recoveries. After a long discussion with Mr. Darcy, we both agreed that half-mourning (which should begin this month on the 17th) will be cancelled. This house has seen enough mourning; it must now be restored to the living. Poor Mrs. Reynolds is in shock! It was she who prompted our conversation by enquiring about the servants' clothes and uniforms for the half-mourning period. When I gave directions to remove the coverings from mirrors and pictures and all other signs of mourning, and to order the servants to revert to their normal liveries, she was so distressed that I insisted she take a seat and a little wine. It took me a full half hour to persuade her that this decision had nothing to do with a lack of respect or affection for the dead, but everything to do with life and living, that without the everyday gloom of Pemberley in mourning, our hearts will mend very much sooner. A few tears followed: Mrs. Reynolds was as fond of Cassie as she is of Annie and feels her loss as deeply as any of us.

Now the poor woman has to explain our uncommon decision to the household (as well as to her counterparts in the houses hereabouts, I dare say), but I care not what they or anyone else thinks—our spirits are already vastly improved, which another six months of mourning could not accomplish. Even on this cold morning, to see the rooms bathed in sunlight again is a balm. My Husband walks with a more determined and sprightlier step, and set out hunting this morning with something like his old enthusiasm. He also talks of setting up a shooting party with your Husband and Mr. Daley. Jane, you have no idea what joy it gives me to hear him talk so! As for me, my heart is easier. I have instructed Mrs. Reynolds to do what she will with the mourning clothes and livery—I have no wish to see them ever again.

Mr. Darcy and I agree that this is the very best way to begin another year: letting the *light* into our lives again, spending more time in the present than in the unalterable past, and looking to the future with hope and optimism. All this was accomplished on the eve of the New Year, just the two of us before a good fire and perfectly at ease, at times in conversation talking of our resolution, at times in pleasurable silence.

And you were never far from my thoughts that evening, dear Jane—my present and future happiness will always depend in large part upon your own. May this New Year bless us all.

Affec.
E. D.

PEMBERLEY
MONDAY, 29th JUNE, 1818

ir,

Miss Anne Elizabeth Darcy, aged four years, three weeks and a day, presents her compliments and regrets to inform you that, as a consequence of undue and unsanctioned horseplay in her Mamma's sitting room (whence she is not allowed unless bidden) an inkwell overturned, its contents spilling upon her Mamma's favourite chair. Miss Darcy also wishes you to know that she was confined to the nursery for the remainder of the day to practise her letters.

Miss Darcy's Mamma would greatly appreciate if as soon as convenient you could arrange for a sufficient quantity of fabric in the very same shade of pale yellow silk to be sent to the upholsterer in Derby who carried out the original work on your behalf. She would be further obliged if you could advise the date when the material is expected to be delivered so that she may arrange for the chair to be taken to Derby.

Miss Anne Elizabeth Darcy deeply regrets the inconvenience this will doubtless entail, and by way of apology and compensation offers you the enclosed pansy, which she picked and pressed herself last spring, and which she trusts will be to your liking.

Yours &c.

Humphry Repton, Esq.
Sloane Street
London

PEMBERLEY

THURSDAY, 9TH JULY, 1818

Dear Jane,

Thank you for the solace your words brought me. Can it really be that almost a year has passed since Cassie's death? Time is very wayward, is it not, and plays devilish tricks upon us. You might tell me it all happened yesterday, or ten years ago—I could as easily believe the one as the other. From having wondered how to endure the endless hours and minutes of every long day, of a sudden we find ourselves one week away from the anniversary of one's world coming to a devastating halt, only to find that life has continued after all: the seasons still come and go, crops are planted and harvested, fruits bottled and jellied, meat pickled and cured. Much to our amazement, we find that we are able to laugh again and enjoy life—hearts can indeed mend and are far more resilient than we expect them to be.

You ask how we plan to spend that day. Neither of us has spoken of it in those terms, though each knows it is in the forefront of the other's mind. It appears that neither of us wishes to be the first to speak of it, as if by keeping silent, the day will never arrive! How strange we mortals are! The absurdity of human behaviour is a subject worthy of serious study, and if our Father had not had five daughters and a Wife in his care, he might have had more time to devote to such a laudable endeavour. (You see how I have successfully evaded answering your question!) In truth, though, apart from attending church and bringing flowers to Cassie's grave, I know not how the day will progress. Should the day be fair, a very long, strenuous walk will be the very thing to occupy *me*. (I wonder if there are any books of etiquette on how Parents should properly comport themselves on the anniversaries of their Children's deaths?)

Miss Annie plays at my feet with her Parsley, the only creature she finds amiable since she discovered the pleasure of shouting "No" at the top of her voice to all and sundry. Her Papa had been spared this spectacle until this very morning, and Miss A. quickly found herself back in the nursery instead of upon her Papa's knee where she is wont to sit at breakfast. I suspect that sitting here with Parsley is a prelude to making amends with her Father, and perhaps we have heard the last of "No"—at least for today. Upon my request she removed her cat from the sofa and the only words I heard were "Yes, Mamma," veritable music to my poor, deafened ears.

Ever yours,
E.D.

Pemberley
Friday, 24th July, 1818

My dear Husband,

I know not whether you hear me when I speak. Mr. Brownley knows not how long it may be until you are with us again; indeed, he cannot fully assure me that you will ever recover. An honest man of integrity, he will not raise false hopes in me, yet much as we both admire his fine character and trust his judgment, part of me (and not a small part) wishes he were more willing to dissemble. He visits twice daily and twice daily his honesty does not allow him to utter the words my heart yearns to hear.

Yet I remain optimistic and so hopeful of a good outcome that I have resolved to keep a journal, this letter to you that, when you awake, you may know all that has happened while you were gone from us. A small writing desk has been moved into your bedchamber by your bed and here I sit with pen and paper. By this means I may also talk to you as always.

I cling to my belief that all *will* be as before, that *together* we will watch with pride as our Daughter (and any other Children we may yet be blessed with) grow into strong, fine people, and that in years to come it will be in our power to look back with gratitude upon many, many happy years spent together, years in which my regard and affection for you only increase. *I shall not be dissuaded from this*.

Will you remember that dreadful day? (Such a conspiracy of fate that your accident should occur on the first anniversary of our darling Cassie's death!) We brought flowers to her grave early that morning, stepped into the church to pray for her, then walked back to Pemberley, that long walk through the woods and alongside the trout stream which we have taken so often. It was a glorious, sunny morning and I recall saying that the sun should have better manners than to show itself on this sorrowful day. You replied that the sun was perfectly polite: how else could it console us but by its warmth? You were right, of course, and I made due apology to the sun.

Despite our long walk and a good breakfast, we were restless. Together we visited Annie in the nursery, where she amused us, quite unintentionally, with a recitation of "Baa, Baa, Black Sheep." It began well enough, then turned into "Sing a Song of Sixpence." Realising her mistake, her efforts to extricate herself only succeeded in muddling her further. To spare her, you gently suggested she take a deep breath and begin again, slowly. "Yes, Papa," she said, in her most serious tone, and taking a deep breath … then another … and another, she burst into a flood of tears—poor Annie was by now so completely befuddled, she had forgotten the first line! Lifting her onto your knee, you dried her tears and comforted her, took down the old *Tommy Thumb's Pretty Song Book*, found the rhyme and began to recite it, softly. Slowly she joined in and by the end her face was wreathed in smiles.

How Annie adores her Papa! She, too, visits you often. The questions are always the same:

"Is Papa dead?"

"No," I reply, "just sleeping to get better after his fall."

"Will he be awake tomorrow?"

"Perhaps, Annie."

Then she asks to be lifted up to kiss your cheek. At bedtime, after her usual prayers for everybody, she asks God would He please take special care of her Papa that night. If in so doing He has insufficient time to watch over herself and Parsley, she will understand. By this time,

Parsley is curled up on her bed dreaming of good mousing on the morrow and quite unconcerned whether or not he is watched over.

I have digressed and will return now to that awful day, that awful anniversary. Strangely, I do not recall clearly how the rest of the day was spent, though we dined as usual and attended Evensong. It was simply a day to be endured, a day of happy memories, sad memories, bitter, angry thoughts, some tears, and perhaps a very small measure of acceptance of the unacceptable.

Following Evensong, you declared a need to pay a call on Mr. Bailey, a tenant of yours whose sheep were sick of some mysterious malady.

"But he lives the far side of Lambton!" I protested, "and look at the dark clouds in that direction! It will be nightfall by the time you return. Surely tomorrow will be soon enough? Or have Barford go if it is such an urgent matter. I beg you to reconsider."

"My love, it is midsummer and will be light for hours yet," you soothingly replied. "In truth, Barford or I could go tomorrow, but this sad anniversary has left me so restless that I welcome the opportunity to go, however thin the excuse for my journey may be. A good ride will give Major some much-needed exercise, and will do much to restore my spirits, I assure you.

"As for the weather, was it not you, dearest Wife, who chastised the sun only this morning? If it should rain at all, it will likely be only a brief summer shower, which will be most refreshing and I shall welcome the soaking. Come now, a smile before I set out. Upon my return, let us have a late supper, and then perhaps you will give me the pleasure of reading aloud some lines of Mr. Cowper, or Mr. Crabbe, if you will—but wait … wait. Some lines of Mr. Cowper's come to me now which I think you will find *à propos:*

> *"Ye fearful saints, fresh courage take,*
> *The clouds ye so much dread*
> *Are big with mercy, and shall break*
> *In blessings on your head.*

"What say you, dearest Lizzy?" you asked with a smile of self-satisfaction at your cleverness.

What could I say? How many times did we read *Light Shining Out of Darkness* after Cassie first became ill? How many times have we read it together during the past year? How often have I read it alone when nettlesome feelings threaten to overwhelm? How could I deny you? It would have been the act of a more selfish Wife than I to have protested further. Much as I wanted you by me, I know that the very great comfort and solace we have in each other cannot reach to those deepest places in our hearts, where reside feelings which mere words are insufficient to describe rightly. I understood your need and, much as I wish that what followed could be undone, I do not regret your decision to set out, nor will you ever hear from my lips any scolding words on the subject. You may depend upon it.

What did follow some two, or perhaps three or more hours later was a storm the likes of which I have seldom witnessed: high winds and heavy rains, jagged forks of lightning and cracks of thunder loud enough to waken Annie. I rushed to the nursery to comfort our Daughter. Parsley had disappeared. Nurse's face was blanched with terror, 'tho' she made a valiant attempt not to show her fear before Annie for which I was thankful. It was some time before I felt able to leave them. Though the storm still raged, Annie, exhausted, eventually cried herself to sleep in my arms and somehow slept through the night. Insisting that Nurse take a restorative glass of wine, I explained that since you had probably taken shelter from the storm and would thus not return until much later after it had passed, she should rest quietly; that I would look in on Annie often while I awaited your arrival.

Settling myself in the library (the place I feel closest to you when you are from home—have I ever told you?) I closed my eyes and fell to thinking about our darling

Cassie. My reverie was interrupted constantly by the sound of falling trees and thunder so that when the knocking began, I first thought it was the storm still raging outside. As the sound became more insistent, I realised that this was some other commotion and got to my feet just as the library door opened to reveal Mrs. Reynolds. Thinking the storm had likely frightened her, I stepped forward to comfort her.

"Come, come, dear Mrs. Reynolds," I began. "Please, sit down and calm yourself. It will be over soon. Let me fetch a glass of wine to help settle you."

"No, no, Ma'am, Mrs. Darcy, it's not the storm—well, it is the storm—but it's not me—it's the stable boy, Tommy Nutt."

"Mrs. Reynolds, calm yourself, I beg you," I said. "I have not the pleasure of understanding you rightly. Are you telling me that Tommy Nutt is afraid of the storm?"

"Yes, Ma'am—no, Ma'am. What I mean is that young Nutt is here."

"Here, Mrs. Reynolds? How do you mean, here?" (By this time, you may suppose, I was in a state of complete confusion.)

"At the front door, Ma'am—or rather, in the hallway—I had him take his boots and coat off, though, Ma'am. It's about Major and he says it's urgent."

"Pray tell young Nutt that Mr. Darcy is from home and that I will tell him to go to the stables upon his return. Tell him to do his best meanwhile and—" At this moment, I recalled that you were riding Major and felt my heart sink faster than a stone in a pond.

"Bring him here quickly, Mrs. Reynolds. There is not a moment to lose."

"But he's soaked through, Mrs. Darcy. And in Mr. Darcy's library, Ma'am?" Her voice trailed away as she looked around the room.

"Mrs. Reynolds, I don't care if he should cause a flood, I must see him this instant—no, never mind." With that, I ran from the room to find the lad standing in a puddle of water, turning his hat round and round in his hands, very ill at ease.

"Beg pardon, Ma'am," he said, gesturing uncomfortably at the water on the floor, lowering his eyes as he spoke.

"No, no, please, reassure yourself, it is of no consequence. Now, please tell me about Major. I must know."

As I was saying this, my mind had leapt ahead, hoping he was about to tell me that, after all, you had decided to take another horse—that Major in a fit of pique at being left behind had broken loose and trampled the rose garden—or run amok in the storm—that since Mr. Darcy's favourite horse was at large, Mr. Darcy would want to know immediately—*anything* but the harsh reality of the truth I dreaded to hear, which was that Major had come home alone a short while ago, frightened out of his wits and making such a commotion in the stable yard that Tommy Nutt had heard him even above the roar of the storm.

Are you surprised that your Wife did not fall into a faint at this dreadful news? Quite to the contrary, she coolly took command, instructing Nutt to ride to Barford's house and tell him to form a search party, which should set out towards Lambton by way of Mr. Brownley, whose services might well be required. Nutt should then return and tend to Major. Mrs. Reynolds meanwhile roused the household and set the kitchen to preparing hot drinks for the rescuers and plenty of hot water. A fire was lit in your bedchamber, bandages were brought, salves and ointments fetched, brandy set out, the bed warmed—everything which could be thought of was made ready for your return. In truth, we were all glad of the occupation to fill the long hours waiting for news.

By this time (I know not the exact hour) the storm had thankfully abated, though the rain continued steadily through the night. With nothing left to do, I took myself to the nursery where Annie slept contentedly with Parsley once again beside her. Their storm was over; my own storm clouds were gathering strength. (I hear you saying, "My dear Lizzy, you read too many novels and become fanciful.") Perhaps, but this is the way I remember the events of that night and shall record them faithfully here.

Towards dawn the party arrived. "Barford, Mr. Brownley, is he alive? Does he live? Is he badly hurt?" I cried, rushing to the door.

"Calm yourself, Mrs. Darcy," said Mr. Brownley. "He breathes, but has lost consciousness and a good deal of blood, I fear. I have given instructions that Mr. Darcy be taken to his bedchamber immediately. Allow me to make my examination, then we will know more, Meanwhile, I beg you to remain calm and hope for the best." With that, he ran up the stairs, leaving me to wait once more.

At last Mr. Brownley reappeared with better news than I had expected: a simple break of the right arm (which he has re-set and which he expects to heal without problem); a badly sprained right ankle; various lacerations (which have been cleansed, and will require no further treatment so long as no infection sets in); much bruising (in particular to the ribs) and a severe concussion. It is this last which gives us cause for anxiety. For a day or two we could be thankful that you were thus spared much pain and discomfort, but tomorrow will be a full week …

It is late and your nurse reminds me of my promise to Mr. Brownley this evening to retire early and rest "… else I shall have two patients at Pemberley, Mrs. Darcy. Once your Husband awakens, you will need all your strength and resources for some time to come."

But first I must write down Mr. Cowper's lines which I find myself reciting silently several times daily—one verse of which was part of our last conversation and is thus especially dear to me. For over a year they have become entwined in our lives and so belong here in this chronicle. Bless dear Mr. Cowper for his solace!

Light Shining Out of Darkness
God moves in a mysterious way,
His wonders to perform;
He plants his footsteps in the sea,
And rides upon the storm.
Deep in unfathomable mines
Of never-failing skill,
He treasures up his bright designs,
And works His sov'reign will.
Ye fearful saints, fresh courage take,
The clouds ye so much dread
Are big with mercy, and shall break
In blessings on your head.
Judge not the Lord by feeble sense,

But trust him for his grace;
Behind a frowning providence
He hides a smiling face.
His purposes will ripen fast,
Unfolding ev'ry hour;
The bud may have a bitter taste,
But sweet will be the flow'r.
Blind unbelief is sure to err,
And scan his work in vain;
God is his own interpreter,
And he will make it plain.
Good night, my dear Husband!

Sunday, 26th July, 1818

Yesterday, not knowing that I had slipped into the bed-chamber behind him, I overheard Mr. Brownley muttering to himself, concerned that bleeding within the head might be causing the delay in your awakening, and wondering if you would be in your right senses if you did finally awaken—might it not be a better thing never to awaken at all?

I quitted the room as silently as I had entered and, feeling the pressure of tight, cold bands of iron around my heart, forced myself to breathe, then breathe again. I shall not believe that you will never return to me, and shall continue to will you to *fight* with all your strength to that purpose.

Jane and Mr. Bingley arrived at noon yesterday, staying but a few hours and taking Annie with them for Elizabeth Cassandra's first birthday tomorrow. It will be good for her to see her Cousins, though she was bitterly disappointed that Parsley was required to remain at home. Nurse and I were given lengthy instructions on the care of her spoiled, pampered cat, then, just as she was about to step into the carriage, Annie decided that after all Mrs. Reynolds was the only proper person to be trusted with such an important matter as Parsley's welfare, and sped off to find her. There is a picture at your side, a self-portrait drawn by your Daughter. "If Papa should awaken while I am gone, please give him this picture that he may remember me."

The Bingleys are well but, as you would imagine, most concerned on your behalf. Mr. Bingley wishes very much to fetch his own physician here, a person upon whom he places great reliance—he feels a second opinion is in order. It was a kind gesture and I thanked him kindly, but feel it an unnecessary step, at least for now. Mr. Brownley has taken care of the Darcy household for a long time and is yet young enough and curious enough to keep up with the latest in medical matters. Upon leaving, Mr. Bingley and Jane made me promise faithfully to call upon them for anything at any time—something I should never hesitate to do, and was able to give them my word wholeheartedly.

At church this morning, Mr. Kirkland offered up prayers for your quick recovery. Everyone there wanted to know how you go on. While I appreciate their kindness in enquiring, it is very wearing to be obliged to acknowledge it over and over again and I was pleased to make my escape from their good wishes to be home. No, I have not put it rightly: I do not mean to sound as arrogant as my words appear. I am exceedingly grateful for the interest and good wishes conveyed. The livelihoods of many people rest in your capable hands, and they must be as anxious as your own Family for your speedy recovery.

Monday, 27th July, 1818

Mr. Brownley informs me that the bruising and swellings have diminished considerably in the past seven days, and that no signs of infection are evident. "A good sign, Mrs. Darcy, a good sign of a strong constitution."

More heartening news is that Major appears none the worse for his experience. Once he was cleansed of the mud, dirt, blood and brambles which covered him, just a few cuts and scratches were to be seen. A lingering lameness had been a little worrying, but by yesterday had thankfully improved; he eats well again and is slowly regaining his usual calm and friendly disposition. Loud noises of any kind troubled him greatly at first but he is becoming more settled with each day that passes.

Barford informs me that young Tommy Nutt rarely leaves the horse's side and deserves much credit for Major's swift recovery. You will, I am sure, wish to reward such devotion. Meanwhile, if the weather stays fair, I shall walk to the stables this afternoon to express my own gratitude. There has been no further rain since Saturday night, but it is still wet and muddy in parts.

Tuesday, 28th July, 1818

No change.

Wednesday, 29th July, 1818

No change.

Thursday, 30th July, 1818

No change, though I should have mentioned previously that Mr. Brownley has instructed the nurses to move your good arm and legs in certain directions several times daily to prevent a wasting of the muscles and to keep the blood flowing in a proper manner.

Friday, 31st July, 1818

Barford asked to see me this morning. Noting that it is the last day of the month today, he wanted to review with me outgoings and estate plans for the coming month. My first thought was to tell him to proceed as he sees fit since he has had the management of the Pemberley estates for longer even than the present Mr. Darcy, but I hesitated. Perhaps it is time that I knew a little of everyday life on the estates upon which our lives depend, life beyond Pemberley's park wall! (My Mother's voice echoed in my mind, "Lizzy, what can you be thinking of? A well-brought-up Lady in your position has no business meddling in affairs which are solely the province of Gentlemen. Mark my words, Miss Lizzy, your Husband will not look upon your interference kindly.")

My own voice replied that my dear Husband has ever treated me as an equal, not a mere accessory, and with that, my Mother was dismissed and Barford was asked to take a seat.

After enquiring after you, he began with an accounting of the storm damage, which made a great deal of mischief among our trees. One of the splendid elms fell into the pond; another has fallen amongst some chestnuts and firs, knocking down one spruce fir, beating off the head of another and stripping two chestnuts of several branches in its fall. Several other trees were also blown down, but I regret the elms more than the rest.

To the house itself, little damage was immediately apparent, but Barford wisely had the roof inspected. Three chimneys were found in such a state as to make it miraculous that they have stood so long, and next to impossible that another such violent storm should not blow them down. These the masons are to repair them speedily in the coming days.

On the Home Farm, it appears that after some fences are mended and a number of roof slates replaced, all will be well. Some sheep escaped through broken fences, but all are now accounted for. The hay was safely got in last month, as you know, and though the hayfields are flattened now, with good weather they may recover in time for a second cut. He is as hopeful for the corn fields, which were likewise flattened. Elsewhere, likewise, there are reports of fallen trees and broken fences, but nothing to cause great concern or expense.

Barford then moved on to monthly receipts and payments, producing two large ledgers each filled with columns of bewildering figures, and explanations of the sort that Harry Dewland had still not yet paid his midsummer quarter rent in full, but had promised the balance owing would be paid on 1st August after *he* had been paid for some sheep he had sold to Arthur Russell.

"Mr. Darcy knows all about it, Ma'am," said Barford. "Russell had some bad luck losing some of his sheep to the fever, and Mr. Darcy, aware that Dewland needed to raise money, asked me to arrange the sale, and to inform Dewland that the balance of the quarterly rent owing could be paid thereafter."

Explanations of even more complicated transactions followed. In truth, I could not follow the half of it, but at the same time could not help but be flattered that Barford should take so much trouble to relate these various matters in such detail to enlighten me, presumably under the misapprehension that I was comprehending every word!

My dear Husband, how do you manage to keep up with it all: the tenants' names, their Wives' and Children's names, the sheep, the crops, the cottages, the churches, the livings, &c., &c.

Lastly, Barford reviewed charitable outgoings, and here I confess myself utterly astonished. On my first visit to Pemberley, I recall Mrs. Reynolds described your Father as "very affable to the poor" and declared (much to my amazement at the time) that "his Son will be just like him … the best landlord, and the best master that ever lived." Now the full import of those words was revealed as, at my insistence, Barford listed names of parishioners and tenants who have been and continue to be beneficiaries of your generous, kind heart: some receive food, others alms, poorer tenants receive bread twice-weekly, tenants are sent produce or meat on the birth of a Child or for a christening. Why did I not know? My question is answered at once: why did I not enquire? My Dear, I am heartily ashamed that I have contented myself merely with bits of sewing for the poor basket and visits to the sick and ailing without seeing or asking about the larger picture right before me had I only bothered to look beyond the small, comfortable world of Pemberley. How like you to do what is right quietly and modestly, leaving lesser mortals to crow about their occasional achievements, which are *nothing* to your everday acts of charity! But, belatedly, my eyes have been opened and I am resolved to make up for my woeful inadequacies. How? I know not yet; I am unable to think beyond our present circumstances. Once you are returned to me—oh! *please*, please let it be soon!

Friday, 7th August, 1818

Your Daughter writes, "*der papa, did you woke we piked blakberrys, annie*"

Jane adds that Annie asks after her Papa each morning and mentions him in her prayers each evening, but does not dwell on the subject for too long and shows no signs of melancholy.

Wednesday, 12th August, 1818

Unannounced and quite unexpectedly, my Father and Kitty arrived after breakfast! It was a welcome surprise nonetheless and I am pleased they are here. Kitty informs me that since they received word of your accident, life at Longbourn has become intolerable: My Mother is distraught and has persuaded herself that I am about to be left a destitute Widow with a Daughter. Moreover, such vast estates *must* be entailed away from the female line.

Her imaginings know no bounds on that score—her favourite is that Lady Catherine will sweep in immediately following your funeral and unceremoniously evict me and our Daughter. You will likely not be surprised to learn that further, this is my own fault for not having produced a Son and Heir. Of course, her imaginings have been retailed throughout the neighbourhood where they have fast become fact. As a consequence, my Mother now receives frequent calls from her sympathetic acquaintance (daily visits from Lady Lucas) *supposedly* enquiring after your health and hoping for good news from Pemberley. The reality, needless to say, is quite the opposite: Each wants to be the very first to hear of your demise and my own destitution in order to be able to rush around the neighbourhood self-importantly with the awful tidings!

(My darling Husband, I rely on you to disappoint them all! Hearing this tale made me laugh heartily for the first time in so very long—I have always found absurdity and preposterousness hard to resist, but it was strange to hear myself laugh again.)

As a consequence of her imaginings, which grew daily more vivid (Kitty continued) my Mother's nerves began to suffer accordingly, until my Father could bear to hear no more, announcing at dinner Saturday last that he would be departing for Pemberley on the morrow. At first quite taken aback, my Mother quickly recovered to say that, despite being quite unwell, she, too, would make the journey regardless of the cost to her own health, whereupon my Father insisted that no, she was far too ill, and with her nerves in shreds under no circumstances would he countenance her health being further compromised by such a long journey. No, she must remain quietly at Longbourn where she would recover more quickly in peace and solitude. Kitty would accompany him since she might be of some material use at Pemberley.

My Mother protested vigorously at being left entirely alone but my Father reminded her that members of her vast acquaintance appear daily at the door to give her comfort, and furthermore, Mary and Mr. Digweed might be prevailed upon to stay at Longbourn during his absence should she wish it. As it happened, she wished for no such thing and left the table in tears complaining bitterly at being so ill-used by her own Family.

Kitty is overjoyed to be here and away from Longbourn, not least because she has hopes of seeing again the curate she met while staying with Jane, I am sure, but when I ventured as much, she blushed prettily and would say no more on the subject. She insists her first intent is to be of help to me in whatever way she can. Her company is most welcome and has lifted my spirits considerably. As you might expect, except at meal times my Father is mostly invisible, but just knowing he is somewhere close by is immensely comforting.

Monday, 17th August, 1818

As a diversion for Kitty, the Norland girls paid us a visit. They were so evidently pleased to see Kitty again, and for her part, Kitty was overjoyed to reacquaint herself with them. (As we know, life at Longbourn for Kitty is … well, we know what life is like for Kitty now that Mary is married, and Mary apparently loses no opportunity on her very frequent visits there to remind Kitty of the superior position of her own married state.) The girls thanked me for the invitation to visit Kitty, and apologised for their absence of late. They did not wish to burden me with visits, or with too many letters, which I might then feel obliged to answer. The girls will stay a week. With Annie at Jane's, it is good to hear conversation and laughter around the house.

Saturday, 29th August, 1818

My love, I am so sorry. Please forgive me. I shall apologise to Mr. Brownley when he comes in the morning—if he comes in the morning, but I shall make amends somehow. My face burns when I recollect my outburst. Now, some hours later, I see that he was attempting to be kind in preparing me for the worst. Poor man, his crime was that, in answer to my usual questions, he said, "Mrs. Darcy, I think we must begin to consider seriously the possibility of your Husband *not* making the recovery we have long been hoping and praying for."

His words cut to my very core, from whence erupted a torrent of red-hot words, which have the power to sear me even now as I recall them, but which I shall not record here. I would not wish you to read them. Suffice to say that first, I rounded on the good physician, putting the entire blame for your prolonged ill-health upon him, then railed at you, my good, dear Husband, for having gone out that day, for leaving me and our Child all alone in the world, &c., &c.—I cannot bear to recount more of the sorry episode. I believe Mr. Brownley must have administered laudanum for next I knew, I was in my bed with Kitty at my side, greatly distressed. Fearing that the very worst had happened I made to rush from my chamber, but in my weakened state Kitty was able to restrain me. "Lizzy, Lizzy," she entreated me, "calm yourself, I beg you. You are not well. You have eaten nothing today—here, take a little broth, then we will visit Mr. Darcy together. You will see for yourself that nothing has changed. My Father has been sitting with Mr. Darcy and would have sent word immediately if we were wanted."

And so it was. We found my Father at your side reading aloud, the sight of which brought tears to my eyes, tears of gratitude for the devotion of my family mingled with tears of sorrow for the pale figure who was my strong, vital Husband, whom I miss to the very depths of my soul.

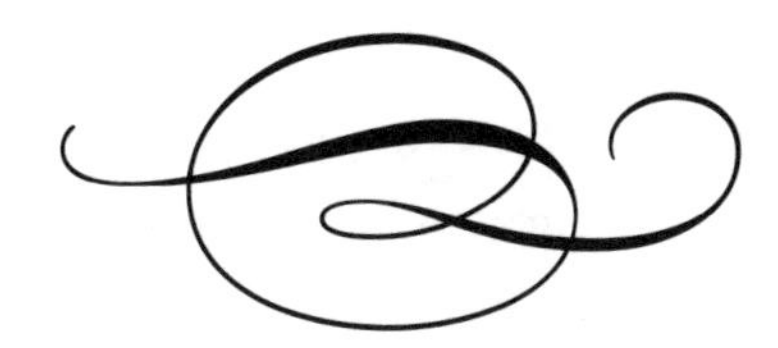

PEMBERLEY

SUNDAY, 30th AUGUST, 1818

Jane, he lives! He is awake! I can scarce believe this is not a dream, but as Mr. Brownley and Kitty and my Father all assure me it is true, I am sure I shall believe it myself before long. Please tell Annie that her dearest Papa has awoken, that he has seen the drawing she left for him, that he longs to see her. Tell her that our Family will be as before, no, better, for our near-loss will surely strengthen our love for one another. Oh, Jane, am I making sense? You will know exactly what to tell Annie and I leave it in your hands to put rightly.

But the particulars. You will want the particulars. Very early this morning, I was awoken by one of Mr. Darcy's nurses knocking at the door, telling me to come immediately. Assuming he had taken a turn for the worse, I ran to his room before she could say another word, and you will imagine my utter astonishment when I tell you that he was sitting up in bed, eyes open, demanding to be told what was going on! (It was his turn to be astonished when he found out how long he had been lying unconscious and that he had given us all great cause for alarm.) I sent for Mr. Brownley instantly and meanwhile attempted to tell my Husband of the storm, the accident, the injuries, his horse, &c., &c. He had no recollection of any of it, but given his seeming comprehension of what I related, I was hopeful of his being of sound mind. Once Mr. Brownley arrived, he, too, was of the same opinion. We are thus reassured that after he has regained full strength (which may well be a matter of several weeks) he will be fully restored to good health. Is that not wonderful news? He was able to take a little broth, then slept for several hours—a harrowing time, for we wondered how long it might be before he woke again—was this merely an aberration? Were our hopes to be dashed? We all breathed a collective sigh of relief when he finally awoke again. (Mr. Brownley advises us to awaken him ourselves, if necessary, and to administer broth frequently to build his strength.)

I have not left his side since and write to you from the little desk I set up in this room an eternity ago. He tires easily but for a few minutes during the wakeful periods, I read from the journal I began shortly after the accident (though omit the most distressing parts which he may read for himself when he is able.)

Mrs. Reynolds brought the good news to church this morning and I ordered the bells to be rung—never have they announced gladder tidings!

A kiss for my darling Annie and my dearest love to you, precious Sister,

E.D.

PEMBERLEY

MONDAY, 31st AUGUST, 1818

Dearest Mamma,

I send this express so that you may know with all that my Husband awoke from his long slumber yesterday morning. Beyond his bodily weakness, which will improve as he is able to take more nourishment, he appears none the worse for the injuries to his head.

Kitty has undertaken to furnish the particulars, but I wanted you to receive the good news from my own hand. I feel sure you will share our great relief, and enormous gratitude for his deliverance.

We are all otherwise well. Annie is at The Great House with Jane. My Father and Kitty have been sources of great strength to me during this time of great difficulty and I have been grateful for their support and good company. Now that we are assured of Mr. Darcy's eventual recovery, I have urged them both not to delay a planned visit to the Bingleys on the 17th. My Father will likely depart for Longbourn from The Great House, but please allow me to ask if Kitty might be permitted to return to Pemberley? It will be some time before Mr. Darcy is quite well again and Kitty's continued presence here will be a great help and comfort to us. It would also thus be in her power to accompany Annie on her journey home. My Father has given his permission, and I hope I may depend on your gracious approbation as well, dearest Mamma.

I trust this letter will find you in restored health. Be assured, Ma'am, of the continued love and respect of your Daughter,

Pemberley

Tuesday, 29th September, 1818

My dear, dear Kitty,

I confess, your wonderful news did not greatly surprise me, but my lack of astonishment is more than compensated by my joy at your happiness. I shall hope to have the honour of meeting your Betrothed before long, though Jane intimated to me after first meeting your curate last year that he would be a worthy partner in life for you. Unlike your Sister Lizzy, Jane is never wrong in these matters and I trust her judgment implicitly. At your second meeting, Jane observed a mutual attraction and was able to further deduce that Mr. Perrot is a man of sense and good manners. Mr. Bingley, cajoled into finding out more as to his character, could find nobody willing to say a bad word against him. Quite to the contrary, wherever his name was mentioned, he was referred to as a man of integrity, who does much good in the neighbourhood without a hint of sanctimony or that superior air sometimes affected by clergymen. And now that you tell me of his love of poetry and keen sense of the ridiculous, I know I shall like my new Brother immensely!

As to money, my love, do not trouble yourself too much, and do not use the lack of money as an excuse to delay your nuptials for too long. While your portion is, sadly, small, I feel certain that Mr. Perrot's prospects must be good, given his intelligence and personable character. With you as his Wife and helpmeet, he will have the confidence, support and the will to make his way in the world. You also have the benefit of your Sisters' connections and Family and I feel certain both Mr. Bingley and Mr. Darcy will wish to assist Mr. Perrot's advancement if they are able.

Shall you be married from The Great House, or from Longbourn? Though you say a long engagement is planned, Miss Annie is anxious to know the particulars. Never having attended a wedding, the news that her beloved Godmother will be married is of very particular interest. Weddings have become a subject of great curiosity since your letter and she has taken to wearing daisy chains in her hair and around her neck, fancying herself very smart—the long-suffering Parsley is similarly bedecked. His role in the proceedings is unclear, but so long as he can continue to sleep undisturbed, he appears content to play whatever part is required.

How very convenient for Mr. Perrot that my Father spared him the inconvenience of a journey to Longbourn to ask for your hand! What news Papa will have when he returns home! (By the bye, my Mother did not reply to my letter requesting that you be allowed to stay longer—perhaps she wrote to you directly? On the assumption that she gave her approbation (in any case, Papa has already agreed) pray do not feel obliged to return to Pemberley on my behalf. Nothing would please me more than that you and Mr. Perrot should come here, but I fear Mr. Darcy is not yet well enough to receive company, so we must postpone that pleasure.

Dear Kitty, I wish you great joy. If you are fortunate to have even half the happiness Jane and I have found in our marriages, you will be a happy woman, and you deserve nothing less.

Kindly present my best compliments to Mr. Perrot, whose acquaintance I look forward to making.

Ever yours,

PEMBERLEY

FRIDAY, 16th OCTOBER, 1818

Dear Lady Ashton Dennis,

How very kind of you to send me "Endymion!" The first words alone brought tears to my eyes:

A thing of beauty is a joy forever:
Its loveliness increases; it will never
Pass into nothingness; but still will keep
A bower quiet for us, and a sleep
Full of sweet dreams, and health, and quiet breathing.

I was naturally put in mind of my darling Cassie; Mr. Keats' sentiments gave me great ease. And later:

... and did give
My eyes at once to death: but 'twas to live,
To take in draughts of life from the gold fount

Of kind and passionate looks; to count, and count
The moments, by some greedy help that seem'd
A second self, that each might be redeem'd
And plunder'd of its load of blessedness.

Since the dark days of Mr. Darcy's accident and his subsequent delivery, I am determined to take in large, daily draughts of life, and to count and count the moments. Mr. Keats immediately joins Cowper and Byron among my favourites and I shall look forward to his future works with great anticipation.

I thank you, too, for your enquiries after my Husband's health. He makes great progress, is able to walk unaided a little further each day, the arm no longer gives him pain and has mended well, and the headaches he suffered upon first awakening have all but gone. His strength increases daily and he has a good appetite.

His disposition, however, is sadly another matter. It is probably natural for a man of his temperament to resent this enforced dependence, but it is quite disconcerting that he should be so ill-tempered; his low spirits often lead him to be curt and sometimes uncivil to those who love him most. Mr. Brownley assures me this is to be expected and will pass once he is strong enough to carry out the normal daily round once more. Let us hope it may be soon. I see the look in Annie's eye as she approaches her Father to sense his mood. I would not wish her to become afraid of him.

I have said far too much. Forgive my ill-manners in unburdening my heart to you—my pen ran away of its own accord and knew not when to stop. I pondered whether to begin this letter afresh, but then recalled dear Eleanor saying how grateful she often was for being able to confide in you unreservedly and without fear. In trusting *her* good judgment I feel confident of *your* discretion.

I have not had the pleasure of a letter from Eleanor these past several months, so am delighted to hear from you that she is in good health in the Bahamas. Twins! What a surprise she must have gotten! Please give her my heartiest congratulations when you next write.

Annie, now four, is quite the little Lady. She has learned almost wholly of her own accord the alphabet and the figures, and reads and spells and recites nursery rhymes for our amusement. Our lessons together are very pleasant and we have today finished a second page of three-letter words. For a treat, her Papa will take her on his lap, and together they find all the o's or any other letter on a page in a magazine or book.

While I am heartily glad that life in Bath is so much to your liking, I am sorry that *your* pleasure denies me *mine!*

Your visits hereabouts have become all too rare and I miss our talks about books and poetry.

Be assured that your thoughtfulness in sending the Keats' verses is sincerely appreciated by your Friend,

Elizabeth Darcy

1819

Pemberley

Wednesday, 20th January, 1819

My dear Mrs. Daley—Margaret, if I may …

Would that any words of mine could offer any real comfort to you on the death of your esteemed Father. Each death in our lives is a personal, lonely experience, and the loss of so kind and affectionate a Parent must be deeply hurtful, more especially as your constant residence with him has given you the more intimate knowledge of his virtues. The raw, burning grief that envelops us as a consequence will not be ignored and while the head whispers that the loved one's passing was a release from worldly ills, the soul aches with a sorrow no balm can assuage.

Yet I can tell you that the red-hot fire of grief will pass. After Cassie's death, I would become very angry when people insisted on telling me this for I did not believe it, not for one moment. The heavy stone that was my heart, the grief, the tears, the loneliness had so completely taken over that they were my whole being, never to depart. Indeed, I did not wish them to depart, but time has a strange way of healing, finally leaving one free to resume one's life, to laugh again and live again without guilt and without dishonour to the departed. In time I hope you, too, will find that to do so is to honour your Father. He would not wish it otherwise, I feel certain.

For my part, I shall remember your dear Father as a good, kind man, who was surely an excellent Father, for he could not otherwise have had a Daughter so loving and solicitous and mindful of his welfare. I hope you will be comforted by the consideration of the little enjoyment he was able to have from the world for some time past, and of the small degree of pain attending his last hours.

I shall not press you to write, but when you are equal to it I hope we shall receive from you as good an account of Mr. Daley and yourself as can be expected in these early days of sorrow.

Yours ever,

Elizabeth Darcy

PEMBERLEY

SATURDAY, 15th MAY, 1819

Dearest Jane,

I have so many things to acquaint you with that I know not where to start … Well, let me begin with the shortest of my announcements: Expect another Nephew or Niece this coming November! Annie professed her delight at first, but with all the innocence of a Child, asked if her new Brother or Sister was going to die like Cassie. She asks the same question thrice daily at least, and whenever it arises, her Papa and I, abetted by Nurse, take as much time as is required to reassure her. We do not wish this fear to be perpetuated and encourage her to love her new Sibling every bit as much as she did her Sister.

Speaking of her Sister, you know that it has long been my wish to make a lasting memorial to Cassie—we have spoken of it so often—and I believe that I have finally come upon the perfect answer (be patient, I shall come to the details in due course, but allow me first to indulge my peregrinations).

While Mr. Darcy was lying unconscious, I had an abundance of time for thinking, and one day when I was feeling particularly low in spirits, I scolded myself out of self-pity by making a list of the material blessings I am privy to each and every day here at Pemberley, not even counting the further benefit I derive from the surrounding villages and farms which form part of the estate:

One large mansion (so large that I am not even aware exactly how many rooms there are, but at least 50)
Stables and horses
Mews with carriages of various kinds
Fish ponds
Duck ponds
Trout streams
Flower gardens
Vegetable gardens
Walled gardens
Orchards
Beehives

Dairy
Piggery
Lumber mill
Corn mills
Ice house
Greenhouses
Fernery
Woods
&c., &c., &c.

By the time I had added to this list the many people who daily make Pemberley—and my life—run so efficiently and smoothly, I felt like a spoiled Child. Barford had previously opened my eyes when we reviewed estate affairs together during Mr. Darcy's indisposition (how quickly I had forgotten my own awe and astonishment (just five years ago!) at the sheer size of Pemberley, and the numbers of people required to properly manage such a household and estate as this). Unlike my own Husband, I had previously not given more than a passing thought to the people whose very existence depended upon the whims of the Darcy Family. No, I had been much too busy with my own affairs, now and then smugly distributing patched clothing to the poor and baskets of food at Christmas. How often and easily I have remarked how thankful I am for my blessings, without really knowing what those many blessings were! Even my own grief at my Daughter's death and my Husband's accident clouded my eyes to the many Families who suffer unkind blows of fate, but because of their situations in life cannot permit themselves the luxury of withdrawing from the world with their sorrow if they are to put food on the table and keep a roof above their heads.

Since that time I have been resolved upon doing something worthwhile for the benefit of not only estate workers and their Families, but also others less fortunate than I. At last, I have come up with a scheme which pleases me exceedingly. Last week, I laid it before Mr. Darcy for the first time, who, you should know, was as impressed with my secrecy as he was with my plan. Together we refined it and here, in short, is what we propose:

A free school is to be set up in Lambton, to be named the Cassandra Darcy School, for all Children up to age 11 years. For Children older than 11, who have the inclination and ability to further their studies, we shall set up scholarships that they may attend other fine schools in Derbyshire without fear of burdening their Families with the costs of their education.

Barford (whom I had previously sworn to secrecy and consulted as to a possible suitable building for my purpose) thinks he knows the perfect place on the outskirts of the village, a former inn on the old coach road which has been empty for some years. Since it belongs to the Pemberley estate, all that was required was Mr. Darcy's consent—freely and generously given, I may say.

Moreover—and this was Mr. Darcy's idea—the outbuildings can be easily converted into a lending library for all, which will be called the Cassandra Darcy Memorial Library. Jane, what do you say? I long for your opinion! Will not these schemes be a fitting memorial for our darling Girl? Most people hereabouts find themselves in Lambton during the week on some business or other, so it is the very spot for a lending library. Both the school and library will be properly set up with a board of governors, or whatever is required (Mr. Darcy will instruct his attorney) and Sir Richard Mansfield has indicated already that he would be delighted to serve in some capacity or other. I have no doubt we shall have no difficulty in persuading others to join us.

The only problem we envisage is convincing villagers and tenants of the wisdom of sending their Children to our school when they might be useful at home or in the fields, especially those who fear their Children knowing more than they do themselves. Mr. Darcy, however, feels certain that a few words from him, or one of his agents, will persuade any reluctant Parents.

In part with that in mind, I have further plans to hold weekly reading and writing classes for the adults, perhaps at the library. I have enlisted the help of the Vicar's Wife, who was at first puzzled by the notion of educating them, wondering aloud whether it might not be safer to leave them in ignorance. Reason at last prevailed and she is now such a keen advocate of the classes that she speaks of them as if the idea were her very own. I am more than pleased to allow her the credit, especially since she has undertaken to find the proper teaching primers, and not least because her Husband will be a valuable ally from the pulpit.

Lastly, there is to be a soup kitchen to feed the poor, also at Lambton, which is so usefully situated. I spoke about this to Margaret Daley recently (have I mentioned that the Daleys are to remove to Mr. Daley's estate at Weldon? While Margaret's Father was still living, they had resided at his house, which will now be sold. I know I have not told you that a Daley Heir/ess is expected in October, for I was only just informed myself.) Anyhow, now that they will be living even closer to us, the Daleys have offered to underwrite both the establishment and weekly costs of the soup kitchen as a memorial to her Father. Is that not delightful, Jane? (I have to admit to noticing a certain irony when I recollect that her Father was a very finicky eater indeed!) In their enthusiasm, the Daleys have even improved upon our plan, and the soup kitchen will encompass a scheme to take food to the sick.

Dear Jane, using my grief to good purpose is a feeling as intoxicating as any wine. I have been quite giddy with joy and anticipation ever since I first summoned the courage to lay before my Husband all that I have just related. Death has not triumphed over us, but has been the means of creating something new, something wonderful, something we shall take great pride in—my dear Daughter will live as long as the school and library stand.

I must now gather up young Annie, who, like her Mother, is anxious to be outdoors on this glorious May morning.

Ever yours,

Elizabeth

PEMBERLEY

SUNDAY, 18th JULY, 1819

My dear Jane,

I have every reason to be exceedingly cross with you, but today being the second anniversary of Cassie's death, I should refrain from such unseemly thoughts. No, I have changed my mind. I am exceedingly vexed. That my own, best-beloved Sister should have been in collusion with my very own Husband is quite insupportable. On the other hand, the result of your conspiracy is so wonderful that you are immediately forgiven, and I congratulate you on your ability to keep a secret so well—we were with you for two whole weeks, with nary a word spoken on the subject!

Mr. Darcy is likewise forgiven. I know that he saved his piece of news for this particular day well aware that it would ease the sorrow of the anniversary. His thoughtfulness and consideration for my welfare never cease to astound me. I shall pass on the good news immediately—thank you for allowing me that privilege.

Work on the school and library progressed well during our absence. Walls and doors have been removed here and added there. Windows have been enlarged, draughts sealed, roof slates repaired, fireplaces opened up, and chimneys swept. Once this work is complete in just a few weeks, all will be whitewashed to present light, airy, but snug surroundings for learning and reading.

A few days ago, we were surprised by a visit from Sir Richard Mansfield, who arrived with his Nieces, Anna and Fanny Norland—as you know, two very fine young women for whom I have the highest regard. The surprise was not at their coming, but the reason for their mission: Fanny Norland, the youngest, has set her heart upon teaching at the school, as has her elder Sister, Anna, who also wants very much to run the library! While having no doubts at all as to their competence, Mr. Darcy felt obliged to enquire whether for young women of their station, such occupation might perhaps be considered unseemly. Almost as if he had expected such a question, Sir Richard stepped in immediately.

"My dear Sir, Mrs. Darcy, much as I appreciate your concern for my Nieces' reputations, I beg you would have no worries on that score. My Nieces are refined young women of good education and exceptional intelligence. In teaching Children at a school founded by no lesser personages than your good selves, they would have outlets for their considerable talents and, furthermore, would be great assets to your institution—if I may say so. Young women today (at least, superior young women with active minds and able bodies) want to do more than sit in idleness until a suitor comes their way—and if any young man thinks the less of my Nieces because they have occupied themselves in useful work, he is a damned pompous snob, Sir (forgive me, Ma'am) and ain't worth having! So, what do you say?"

Of course, we accepted immediately and with the greatest pleasure. The Children could have no better teachers and will be in the best of hands. Of course, I know it will not be for very long—while their fortunes may be small, they are both attractive, intelligent and well-connected, and will eventually make good matches, I am sure, but for the time being the school will be off to a fine beginning with teachers of such quality. The school year starts in September after the harvest is brought in and in the meanwhile, the Norlands will begin preparing lessons and lists of supplies they will need.

Jane, how exciting all this is! And I do believe that Mr. Darcy is just as enthused as I am. Needless to say, the school and library are the talk of the neighbourhood. Very little opposition has been encountered, and that from people who have had schooling themselves, if you please! Do you recall my ever mentioning a Mr. and Mrs. Randall? He is the vicar at Oakley. Now that Sir James Steventon resides in Bath, we see very little of them, thankfully, for they are not much liked in our circle. In short, they are a smug, arrogant pair, full of pretensions to the sort of contrived elegance I abhor and for which they are ill-equipped, having neither taste nor judgement. Well, Mrs. Randall was overheard saying to our vicar's wife, Mrs. Kirkland, that while she was not greatly surprised by the news of our school and library (given that Mr. Darcy had married so far beneath himself) she felt that it was a highly questionable enterprise for persons of our rank in society. Indeed, her opinion on the subject was so strong, she had enjoined her Husband to preach of the dangers of educating the lower classes next Sunday at Oakley! Feeling very sure of herself, she was allowed to continue in this vein for some time until Mrs. Kirkland, who could stand to hear no more, interrupted, saying calmly, "So, am I to understand then, Mrs. Randall, that I should not count upon *your* assistance with the reading and writing classes *I am arranging* this autumn? For myself, I consider it an *honour and privilege* to be associated with such a worthwhile enterprise—as well as my *Christian duty*—but you must do as you see fit. Good day to you, Ma'am." With that, she turned on her heel, leaving Mrs. Randall open-mouthed and quite speechless (a rare occurrence).

As Barford and Mr. Darcy go about, they are receiving many enquiries about the classes, and Mrs. Reynolds has been asked by several of the lower household servants if they, too, might be permitted to learn to read and write.

We had thought to meet with much more resistance, and I must say that this present interest is immensely gratifying.

But now I really must write to Kitty.

E.D.

PEMBERLEY

SUNDAY, 18th JULY, 1819

Darling Kitty,

You may indeed wonder why I find myself in such good spirits on this unhappy day. The answer is, my dear Sister, upon your account!

Let me relate the whole story. I think you know that we were at The Great House for two weeks recently with Jane, where we at last made the acquaintance of Mr. Perrot. We met on three occasions altogether—such a very nice Gentleman, Kitty, but you know that already, of course. While we were there, completely unbeknown to me, Mr. Darcy contrived a private meeting with Mr. Perrot, abetted by Jane and Mr. Bingley. I was not to be informed until the outcome was clear, Mr. Darcy wishing to spare me any disappointment should his plan not meet with the success he hoped for.

You know, I am sure, that Mr. Darcy's estate includes several livings. Quite recently one became vacant, the incumbent, a Widower, having retired and gone to live with his Sister in Derby. Mr. Darcy took it upon himself to talk to Mr. Perrot (not mentioning the living) thereby determining his suitability. Duly impressed, Mr. Darcy had a second, private interview with him, following which, Mr. Perrot rode to Boxwood Magna, found everything to his liking, and now it is all happily settled! Mr. Darcy's only conditions were that Mr. Perrot's preferment remain a secret until the anniversary of Cassie's death when he would impart the news to me, and that I should be allowed the privilege of telling you. You will see from the date that I have lost no time in writing; indeed, I shall send this express that your happiness is delayed not a moment longer than necessary.

I should have mentioned earlier that Boxwood Magna is but 25 miles from Pemberley, and perhaps 40 miles from Jane. Mr. Darcy proposes that we visit the vicarage soon with Barford and see what repairs may be required before your arrival. Neither of them has visited there in some time but recall the vicarage as pleasantly situated and well-proportioned with a large, sheltered glebe adjoining. Once we have made our inspection, I shall be able to give you more particulars.

Dear Kitty, how happy you will be! There can be now no further reason to postpone your wedding. I dearly look forward to having you close by. When I came to Pemberley almost seven years ago, it did not enter my head that I might be so very fortunate as to have one of my Sisters in the vicinity, and now I shall have two! I feel quite giddy with anticipation.

Oh, I almost forgot! To add to my joy, a letter from Georgiana just now received announces that she is at last with Child. How will I bear so much happiness?

With affection,

PEMBERLEY

THURSDAY, 25th NOVEMBER, 1819

My dear Aunt Gardiner,

It gives me unimaginable joy to tell you that we were blessed with a fine little Boy at two o'clock in the morning of Saturday, the 18th last. He is a fine, sturdy Infant, perfect and lovely, with an abundant mop of brown hair and large brown eyes. I fancy—and Jane agrees—that he takes after the Bennets; Mr. Darcy disagrees strenuously, asserting he has the Darcy forehead.

Jane was at my side and a great source of encouragement and support throughout. I am filled with gratitude that I was so mercifully dealt with, and am making a speedy recovery; indeed, I am feeling so much recovered and in such good spirits that I hope Brownley, who comes tomorrow, will permit me to quit my bed earlier than the usual two weeks—lying here only makes me fidget and fret and I long for fresh air and exercise. Jane will not countenance my getting up without permission, fearful that I may injure or overtire myself. Nothing I say will persuade her otherwise, so here I lie, but occupy my time usefully in writing to you, dear Aunt.

Oh, but perhaps I am not quite right in the head, for I see I have quite forgot to tell you his name! Since before even Annie was born, it was our intention to name a Son James Fitzwilliam (to honour his paternal Grandfather and Father). So it came as something of a surprise that when Mr. Darcy first set eyes on his newborn Son, he announced that he wanted to change the name we had long ago settled upon. Feeling just a little wronged (for we had always chosen our Children's names together) I looked at him expectantly, trying not to show my hurt at his capriciousness.

"My dear Lizzy, away with that pained look on your lovely face!" he began, with just a hint of a smile about his lips. "Just listen to my proposal. If you are quite against it, he shall be James Fitzwilliam and that'll be the end of it. I assure you I shall love him (and his Mother) every bit as well as if I had had my own way and he were named Bennet."

"Bennet?" I did not yet understand.

"Yes, Bennet Fitzwilliam to be exact, though we would probably call him Ben, I think. Does not that sound well?"

"Bennet … Ben?"

"My love, you are tired and not understanding me rightly. My intention was not to confuse you, but to honour *your* Family, and your Father in particular! Perhaps you have now been so long a Darcy you have forgot you were once Miss Elizabeth *Bennet* of Longbourn in the county of Hertfordshire?"

Indeed, so I was. I had not forgot, but Miss Elizabeth Bennet is a creature I scarcely know any longer. How very far away she seems! How little she knew of life, all the while congratulating herself on her clever perception and insight into the world and its ways! Glimpses of her may still be seen occasionally: when the first warm day of summer compels her to run through the woods, not caring who sees her; or when in company she is obliged to suppress her laughter at some absurdity or other, daring herself not to catch her Husband's eye, who knows exactly what she is about.

Ah, yes, Fortune has smiled upon that girl, bestowing upon her so many gifts: a marriage based on an ever-deepening, mutual affection; the love of a good, kind Man; the great joy of Children, Family and dear Friends;

freedom from want; the strength to endure loss; and the good sense to appreciate her charmed life.

My good fortune, dearest Aunt, continues with the pleasure afforded by our anticipation of your visit at Christmas. Mr. Darcy and I agree that is much too long since we saw you last at Pemberley. What a merry party we shall be: Darcys, Bingleys, Bennets and Gardiners—and now Perrots—all together! And as the old year comes to a close, let us raise our glasses in gratitude for the many blessings bestowed upon us, and for those yet to come.

Affectionately yours,
Elizabeth D.

P.S. My Husband has requested the honour of informing my Mother of the arrival of her Grandson. I am more than happy to oblige him.

Finis

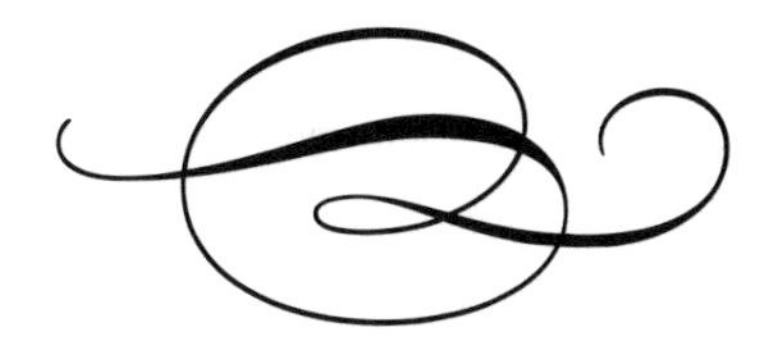

Resources

In addition to those resources already listed in *Letters from Pemberley*, the following books were also very useful:

A Lady of Distinction. *Regency Etiquette: The Mirror of Graces (1811)*. Mendocino: R.L. Shep, 1997.

Blum, Stella. *Ackermann's Costume Plates: Women's Fashions in England 1818–1825*. New York: Dover Publications, 1978.

Booth, Bradford A. *Pride and Prejudice: Text, Background, Criticism*. Harcourt, Brace & World, 1963.

Foreman, Amanda. *Georgiana, Duchess of Devonshire*. HarperCollins, 1998.

Hibbert, Christopher. *Nelson: A Personal History*. Penguin Books, 1995.

Lasdun, Susan. *Making Victorians: The Drummond Children's World 1827–1832*. London: Victor Gollancz, 1983.

Morley, John. *Regency Design: Gardens, Buildings, Interiors, Furniture*. New York: Harry N. Abrams, 1993.

Pollock, Linda. A *Lasting Relationship: Parents and Children Over Three Centuries*. Hanover: University Press of New England, 1987.

Shep, R.L. *Federalist and Regency Costume: 1790–1819*. Mendocino: R.L. Shep, 1998.

Vickery, Amanda. *The Gentleman's Daughter: Women's Lives in Georgian England*. New Haven and London: Yale University Press, 1998.

Jane Austen Societies

United Kingdom

The Jane Austen Society
Carton House
Redwood Lane
Medstead, Alton
Hampshire GU34 5PE

United States

The Jane Austen Society of North America
106 Barlow's Run
Williamsburg, VA 23188

Canada

The Jane Austen Society of North America
105–195 Wynford Drive
Toronto
Ontario M3C 3P3

Australia & New Zealand

The Jane Austen Society of Australia
26 Macdonald Street
Paddington, Sydney
NSW 2021

About the Author

Born in Palestine, Jane Dawkins grew up in Wilton, a small country town in Wiltshire, neighbouring county to Jane Austen's Hampshire. Dawkins now resides in Key West, Florida, with her husband and the three most wonderful Golden Retrievers in the entire world.